The door to her parents' bedroom was wide open.
A narrow strip of light from one of the windows
angled across the neatly made bed.

She hesitated, standing in the doorway, and all at
once she was frightened; they never left the door open
at night.

"Mama?" Her voice was swallowed up by the
suffocating stillness of the empty room. She moved
closer to the doorjamb, holding on to it as she
reached up along the wall, her fingers searching
almost frantically for the light switch.

A soft click.

The darkness remained.

The lights were

THRILLERS BY WILLIAM W. JOHNSTONE

THE DEVIL'S CAT (2091, $3.95)

The town was alive with all kinds of cats. Black, white, fat, scrawny. They lived in the streets, in backyards, in the swamps of Becancour. Sam, Nydia, and Little Sam had never seen so many cats. The cats' eyes were glowing slits as they watched the newcomers. The town was ripe with evil. It seemed to waft in from the swamps with the hot, fetid breeze and breed in the minds of Becancour's citizens. Soon Sam, Nydia, and Little Sam would battle the forces of darkness. Standing alone against the ultimate predator — The Devil's Cat.

THE DEVIL'S HEART (2110, $3.95)

Now it was summer again in Whitfield. The town was peaceful, quiet, and unprepared for the atrocities to come. Eternal life, everlasting youth, an orgy that would span time — that was what the Lord of Darkness was promising the coven members in return for their pledge of love. The few who had fought against his hideous powers before, believed it could never happen again. Then the hot wind began to blow — as black as evil as The Devil's Heart.

THE DEVIL'S TOUCH (2111, $3.95)

Once the carnage begins, there's no time for anything but terror. Hollow-eyed, hungry corpses rise from unearthly tombs to gorge themselves on living flesh and spawn a new generation of restless Undead. The demons of Hell cavort with Satan's unholy disciples in blood-soaked rituals and fevered orgies. The Balons have faced the red, glowing eyes of the Master before, and they know what must be done. But there can be no salvation for those marked by The Devil's Touch.

NIGHT WHISPER

BY PATRICIA WALLACE

ZEBRA BOOKS
KENSINGTON PUBLISHING CORP.

ZEBRA BOOKS

are published by

Kensington Publishing Corp.
475 Park Avenue South
New York, NY 10016

Copyright © 1987 by Patricia Wallace

Second printing: February, 1990

Printed in the United States of America

For Andy, as always

Prologue

December 1960

Something had woken her.

A noise? She listened but heard only the soft whisper of the wind rustling through the branches of the pepper tree outside her bedroom window.

She sat up, careful not to make the bedsprings squeak, and looked around the room. She could make out, in the pale light cast by the moon, the familiar shapes of her doll house and the hobby horse that she was too big for, but refused to give away.

A sudden clanking sound, from outside.

The gate. Someone was at the gate.

She got out of bed quickly, curious now, and went to the window, pushing aside the billowing curtains and pressing her face against the screen.

A dark shape disappeared behind the trees at the end of the path, and she could hear, faintly, the sound of gravel being crunched underfoot.

Whoever it was . . . was running down the drive-

way, away from the house.

The door to her parents' bedroom was wide open. A narrow strip of light from one of the windows angled across the neatly made bed.

She hesitated, standing in the doorway, and all at once she was frightened; they never left the door open at night.

"Mama?" Her voice was swallowed up by the suffocating stillness of the empty room. She moved closer to the doorjamb, holding on to it as she reached up along the wall, her fingers searching almost frantically for the light switch.

A soft click.

The darkness remained.

The lights were out.

She was certain that they were downstairs.

She closed her eyes and envisioned them in the kitchen, a candle between them on the table, their faces lit by the flickering glow. Talking softly.

(Then why couldn't she hear them?)

Father was outside, then, at the fuse box. . . .

(No! Not outside!)

No, they were just sitting quietly, safely, in the kitchen, because they didn't want the sound of their voices to wake her.

The stairs were in total darkness, too far from any window to catch even a hint of light.

With a hand on each banister, she started down.

Halfway, she stepped in something wet, and she had to grab tightly onto the railing to keep from falling. Then, standing on one foot, she wiped the wetness onto her pajama leg, shuddering at the slimy feel of it between her toes.

There was a smell, too, which she couldn't identify, but it was familiar, in a way, and she knew she had smelled it somewhere before.

She took a deep breath and continued downward.

When she reached the turn in the stairway, she could see the front door framed on three sides by slivers of light. The door was ajar.

Never was the door left unlocked.

("The house is too secluded," her father had said, "we're so far back from the road. Someone could break in . . . and no one would hear a thing.")

She sank down until she was sitting and wrapped her arms around her knees, hugging them to her as she stared at the door, trying to make sense of it.

They're on the porch, she told herself, just outside the door. . . .

(No, please . . . not outside.)

She sat on the stairs, unable to go any farther, and waited.

She was still sitting there, tears streaming down her face, when they found her.

By then morning had broken through the windows, and she had seen the reddish-brown stain on her pajamas, the flakes of dried blood between her toes, and she remembered the hot, thick smell of

9

blood from the times her father had killed a chicken for their supper.

No one had to tell her what any of it meant.

"Paige, honey," a voice said softly after a while, "you'd better come along with me."

One

May 1986

Paige Brown injected the wound with xylocaine, the needle cleanly piercing the lacerated flesh.

Beneath the cover of the sterile drape, the patient snored, his breath ripe with the smell of beer and vomit. A bar fight, and he had won, according to the police, but his opponent had struck him with a broken bottle, laying open his face.

Irrigating the wound, she studied the jagged edges of torn skin; it would not be a simple suturing job. Normally she would call for a plastic surgeon to consult on a facial injury of this complexity, but it was 2 A.M. and the man was a regular in the emergency room, his face already scarred from prior encounters with barroom justice. And the surgeon on call tonight was, she knew, more interested in making beautiful people more beautiful than in repairing battle wounds.

She probed the ravaged tissues for slivers of glass and then moved away from the gurney to look, for a second time, at the man's x-rays, narrowing her eyes

as she searched for any fragments she might have missed.

"Okay," she said finally, and turned to the nurse. "Let's see if we can undo what man hath wrought."

An hour later she watched as the patient, flanked by two of the city's finest, was taken, handcuffed, out of the emergency room. She shook her head and turned away.

"A quiet night?" Alex Ryan stood in the doorway to the inner office, a wry smile on his face.

"Depends on your definition of quiet." Paige maneuvered past him and went to the desk to finish the chart.

"How about . . . quiet for a Friday night . . . with a full moon?"

She looked up. "Is it really?"

"What? A full moon or a Friday night? Of course, it's really Saturday morning, isn't it? But yes, there is a full moon, there is always a full moon, it's just that sometimes you can't see all of it."

Paige smiled. "What *are* you doing here at this ungodly hour?"

"I wanted to see you before you left." He sat on a corner of the desk. "You know, going away like this is going to take a little of the wind out of our whirlwind romance."

"The word 'becalmed' comes to mind."

Alex nodded thoughtfully. "I can fix that; come home with me when you get off duty. We'll let everyone think that you've gone off to . . . where is it? Middle-of-nowhere, California?"

"Tranquility."

"Tranquility. Sounds . . . quaint."

She raised her eyebrows. "Do I detect a trace of big city superiority, Dr. Ryan?"

"Never mind. Anyway, what is it they say about going home again?"

"I'm not trying to."

"Aren't you?" His eyes searched hers with an intensity that countered the casual tone of his voice. "Then why are you going?"

Paige didn't answer.

"I wish you'd let me help you."

"As a psychiatrist?"

He shook his head. "As your friend."

"You're a good friend, Alex, but . . . this I have to do myself."

"*What* do you have to do?"

"It's not easy to explain."

"You know, Paige, when they say 'Physician, heal thyself,' no one expects you to take it literally."

"It's not—"

The sudden ringing of the emergency line interrupted them and a moment later the nurse tapped at the door.

"Motorcycle accident," the nurse said.

The motorcyclist was lucky; he'd been wearing a helmet.

"God damn it, it hurts."

Paige looked at the boy's face and nodded. "I'm sure it does." She injected xylocaine subcutaneously in the bend of the elbow, preparatory to performing a

cutdown to establish an intravenous line.

The patient was shivering. One of the nurses had cut off his jeans and T-shirt, and he lay exposed, his pale thin body oddly childlike under the fluorescent lights. A road burn, beaded with pinpoints of blood, covered his left side from shoulder to midthigh.

"Cover him," she said to anyone listening.

She picked up the scalpel from the cutdown tray and made an incision, slicing through the skin, exposing the cephalic vein. Her hands moved quickly, tying off the vein with 5-0 silk.

"Give me an eighteen-gauge needle," she instructed the nurse. A precise flick of the scalpel opened the vein and she inserted the needle, securing it with a second ligature. In less than a minute, she had the IV in and running. She closed with interrupted sutures and then covered the incision with a sterile dressing.

"Okay." She nodded at the nurse and stepped back from the gurney, peeling off her surgical gloves. "Increase his oxygen to six liters per minute. I want stat blood gases, and call the lab to see what happened to the CBC. . . . It should've been back by now."

"Yes, doctor." The charge nurse wrote rapidly.

"And get Radiology back down here . . ." Paige moved to the head of the gurney to make way for the cardiology tech, and then touched the boy gently on the shoulder. "Hang in there," she said.

His eyes fluttered open, and she saw the bewilderment there, the surprise of a child who hadn't known he was playing with fire until his fingers were burned. "Damn it hurts," he said.

14

There was no answer for that.

At ten to six the motorcyclist was admitted to ICU and the emergency room was quiet again.

"Dr. Ryan said to give you this." The unit secretary gave her a note written on a prescription blank. "And this," she said, handing over a manila envelope, "was left at the desk for you during the day shift."

Alex's note was brief and to the point: *Paige: You'll miss me. Call when it becomes unbearable. Alex.*

She smiled, hesitated, then crumpled the note and threw it away.

Her name was printed on the manila envelope in big block letters, the kind of anonymous printing she associated with unpleasant news. She'd had more than her share of unsigned mail; at least once a year some enterprising reporter would include the deaths of her parents in a recounting of unsolved murders, and she would be inundated with warnings and confessions and an occasional threat.

This time it was a request for an interview from a writer who was compiling a book of survivors of violent crime. Since she had never talked to the press, she was, the writer claimed, an ideal subject.

She tore the letter into small pieces.

Part of surviving, she had come to believe, was knowing when to close ranks.

"Dr. Brown?"

Paige turned. The nursing supervisor, clipboard in hand, stood in the doorway. "Yes?"

"They need you to pronounce a patient up on four."

The fourth floor housed the oncology unit.

"All right," she said, trying to keep her voice neutral. It was the part of her job that she hated most: the examination of a lifeless body, the abandonment of hope, the absolute finality of death.

She had yet to learn acceptance.

The patient was a ten-year-old girl with brain cancer. The girl's head was misshapen from where the expanding malignancy had displaced the brain, forcing the tissue through the intracranial openings of the skull.

Central herniation syndrome with symmetric bilateral tissue displacement, according to the diagnosis. The clinical definition, precise as it was, gave no indication of the pain the girl must have endured before slipping into a coma.

Paige placed the stethoscope on the almost skeletal chest and listened for a full minute. When she straightened she nodded at the nurse, who wordlessly handed her the chart. As she took it, she saw that the girl's bony knees were scabbed and she wondered when it had been that the child had run and fallen. Had death been quick, then?

She signed the chart, aware that her hands were shaking.

"Thank you, doctor," the nurse said.

*   *   *

The night, at last, was over.

Coming out of the filtered hospital air into the balmy morning was invigorating, especially after working a twenty-four-hour shift. That this was her last such shift for the next month made it even better, and the exhaustion which had plagued her in recent days began to slip away.

The warmth of the sun had never felt so good.

An hour later, Los Angeles disappeared from her rearview mirror.

Two

Noah Clayton turned off the paved road onto Pine Lane, slowing the patrol car when he saw her.

Missy Prentice stood dead ahead, in the middle of the road, waving and flapping her arms. Her gray hair, usually restrained in a thick braid, seemed to have a life of its own, waving snakelike around her head.

An elderly Medusa in flannel nightclothes.

He radioed his location to dispatch as he pulled to the side of the road, watching as Missy gathered her robe around her and hurried toward him, her slippers kicking up little clouds of dust.

"Morning," he said, getting out.

"Sheriff, they're at it again."

"Who's at what?"

She clutched at his sleeve and began to pull him in the direction of her house.

"The garden this time," she said, as if he knew what she was talking about; she hadn't, to the best of his knowledge, reported any prior incidents. "The bastards got no respect for living things."

"No?" Her eyes were a little wild, he noted, the

whites showing clear around. A vein throbbed at her temple, dark blue beneath parchment skin.

They went around the side of the house, and as they neared the garden, she let go of him to rush ahead. She stopped at the neatly tilled border and whirled to face him.

"See?"

He saw.

A giant tossed salad.

Tomatoes trampled, their seeds spilling into the dark earth. Radishes and green onions uprooted. Zucchini stomped. Embryonic ears of corn twisted off the stalks and shucked, left to dry in the morning sun. Cucumber, bean, and cabbage plants pulled out of the ground and strewn across the lawn.

She waved a broken radish at him. "I want something done about this."

He nodded. Missy was a churchgoing woman, but he knew that she would not be satisfied to leave vengeance to the Lord. "Any idea who might—"

"Kids." She spat the word out.

Noah squatted for a closer look at the dirt, but there were no clear footprints that he could see. Whoever had done this had taken care not to leave any tracks. "You didn't hear anything? Any noises?"

"Just how much noise do you think a tomato makes when it's squashed?"

Noah sifted the cool dirt through his fingers. "Well, if it was kids, I can't think of many who could do all this and keep their mouths closed throughout. Kids are pretty noisy when they're up to no good." He straightened and brushed the dirt from his hands.

"Maybe." The sour look on her face suggested she

20

didn't buy his reasoning.

"All right," he said, "why don't you get dressed and come on down to the office to file a report?"

"I'll file the report," she said, "if that's what it takes to get some action, but I want someone to take pictures of this. This time," she said fervently, "they've gone too far."

Noah walked back toward the cruiser, taking his time, studying the other houses along the road. None of them, he knew, would have a clear view of Missy's garden—there were too many trees and the houses were set far apart—but people slept with their windows open this time of year, and maybe somebody had heard *something*.

This time.

There had been other reports of malicious mischief and vandalism in the past few weeks: a fire set in an empty oil drum behind the gas station, a couple of windows shattered at the school, telephone wires cut, rows of mailboxes knocked off their posts, paint splashed on cars.

Anonymous, random acts. There were no witnesses and no suspects.

Nor was anyone overly concerned, except those directly affected, and even they were more annoyed than anything else, willing, for the most part, to pass it off as some kind of a prank.

Then, night before last, someone had nailed a gutted skunk to the door of Bucky's Tavern. Written, in blood, were the words "dead meat." The entrails were in a neat little pile below the mutilated carcass.

That changed things.

The hostilities had escalated.

And now this . . . not as gruesome, but inherently more dangerous. The tavern had been closed, a confrontation was unlikely. But what if Missy Prentice *had* heard noises, and had gone out to investigate? The potential for violence was undeniable.

Still, if there was a pattern, he failed to see it. Method of operation, seriousness of the offense, choice of victims—what, after all, did Missy have in common with Bucky Hightower? None of it held together in his mind. In fact, the very diversity of the incidents suggested to him a calculated effort to confuse.

And now to frighten. Only who would want to frighten an old lady?

"Damn," he said.

Three

"Oh my God." Ellen Brown Wyatt halted in the doorway and looked into the living room of what was once her brother's home. The movers had been and gone. Even though she knew of Paige's plan to stay here, seeing furniture in the house which had remained empty for so many years gave her something of a shock. "Oh . . ."

The morning sunlight slanted through the venetian blinds, and dust danced in the quickening air.

Martin went from window to window, opening them wide. "Come on in, Ellen," he said.

She couldn't move. Tears gathered at the corners of her eyes; she made no attempt to wipe them away. This room . . . so many memories . . .

"Ellen?"

Hearing the concern in her husband's voice, she turned to face him, to reassure him that she was all right, but as she turned she thought she saw something move, in the corner near the fireplace, and she gasped, her hand leaping to her throat.

Instantly, Martin was by her side. "What is it?"

She shook her head, feeling foolish, and looked at

23

him, then down at his hand, which had encircled her wrist. Was he taking her pulse? Had she alarmed him that much? "I thought I saw something," she said, being purposely vague.

"Something?"

"A shadow, or . . ." She smiled weakly and freed her arm from his grasp. "I'm fine." To prove it, she took a few steps into the room, stopping by the couch and running her hand across the fabric. "Nice."

When she turned she saw that Martin was still regarding her with his "clinical assessment" look. It was a look she had grown quite familiar with since her first attack last fall. Being married to a doctor had certain disadvantages, she'd discovered then; she was under constant surveillance and had a feeling that he considered her almost as a ticking bomb, ready to go off without warning.

"I'm really fine," she repeated, as much for her own benefit as for his.

"I'll take you home if you want."

"No, no . . ." She took a deep breath and surveyed the room. "I want everything to be ready when Paige arrives."

There really was not much to do.

Fresh linen on the bed, clean towels in both bathrooms, light bulbs in the fixtures.

She unpacked dishes, washed them, and put them away in otherwise empty cabinets. The few groceries she'd brought, likewise looking forlorn, were clustered together on a single shelf in the shiny new refrigerator.

24

She set an arrangement of flowers—daisies, baby's breath, and red carnations—on the kitchen table.

The house still felt empty to her.

Ellen watched anxiously as Martin held the phone to his ear and tapped the switch hook several times in rapid succession.

"Works fine," he said, hanging up.

"It wasn't a minute ago."

"I'll check the connections outside." He hesitated. "Why don't you sit down for a while? You look a little shaky."

"I'm—" The word stuck in her throat, and she shook her head impatiently. "I don't want Paige to be here all alone without a phone."

"Relax, Ellen, I'll take care of everything."

When Martin had gone, she returned to the living room and stared uneasily at the corner where, twenty-six years before, the Christmas tree had stood. Even now she could see it . . . tiny silver ornaments and blue—only blue—lights.

In the attic of her own home, the packages she'd gathered from under that tree, their wrappings now faded and brittle with age, still waited for a day she'd never thought would come.

But it had come, hadn't it?

For the first time since that terrible morning, Paige was coming back to the house where her parents had died.

Four

Although she was anxious to get to the library, Felicity O'Hara slowed as she neared the crosswalk. There were cars coming from either direction and she did not want—could not stand—anyone stopping for her. Walking in front of idling vehicles made her nervous.

She wasn't afraid that they would run her over; what she wanted to avoid was anyone *looking* at her. It bothered her in an elemental way to feel herself the object of someone else's attention. Being on display, even for the few seconds it took to cross a street, made her feel vulnerable and exposed.

Not that there was much to look at—she was far too plain. Reddish-blond hair that could only be called strawberry blond if it had been a bad year for strawberries, brown eyes, almost nonexistent eyelashes, and a pale complexion given to uncontrollable blushes at inopportune moments.

Felicity peered into a storefront window and waited for the cars to drive past. There were, she

27

thought irritably, an awful lot of peole out and about for a Saturday morning. Watching the reflections in the window, she noticed a yellow station wagon—the Andersons'?—make a second loop around the traffic circle which marked the center of town.

She groaned and looked at her watch; it was five after ten. Five minutes late, then.

Would he wait?

The station wagon made a third go round, inching along this time.

Was the driver lost?

"No one could get lost in a town this size." The sound of her voice surprised her. Talking to herself was a habit she thought she'd gotten out of. She could feel the warmth rising in her face.

Her image wavered in the glass.

Would he wait?

She hurried up the library steps, head lowered, not wanting to look for him among the small crowd gathered by the door. Although it was now a quarter after ten, none of the patrons complained about her tardiness, nor did anyone comment when, trying to unlock the dead bolt, she dropped the keys twice.

She finally pushed the door open and held it for the others, wishing that she could smile at them to show her gratitude for their patience, but by then her face was flaming hot, and she could not make herself meet anyone's eyes. Instead she fussed with the door itself, as if it, and not she, had somehow delayed the opening.

28

Even with eyes averted, she knew when he passed by her.

The checkout area was on a raised platform, which afforded her an excellent vantage point; she had an unobstructed view of all four reading areas.

He always chose the sun room.

It was the smallest of the cubicles, with barely enough space for the two chairs and narrow low table which had somehow been wedged in. Not the most comfortable place for research, she would think; when he had his papers, books, and notes spread out, there was hardly enough room for *him*.

Maybe that was why he liked it. Certainly no one had ever interrupted his work.

Whatever it was. Since he had never asked her for assistance, she had no idea what he was working on. He had, at one point, spent considerable time going through rolls and rolls of microfilmed newspapers, but what he had been looking for, or what he'd found, she hadn't a clue. All she knew was that every Saturday for the past seven months he had arrived at the library at ten and worked steadily until closing at four. And he never checked any books out.

That she found intriguing.

As indeed she found him.

He was not tall, perhaps five-eight, but nicely built, his slim frame well-muscled, and he dressed casually, today in chinos and a plaid short-sleeved shirt. Dark hair, cut fairly short, a strong masculine face, and hypnotic, smoky blue eyes that promised a

kind of sensual oblivion.

Felicity imagined that looking into those eyes would be like drowning.

She fanned herself absently, watching him, unable to turn away.

If he was aware of her scrutiny, he gave no sign.

Five

Bucky Hightower scowled, looking at the bloodstains. He scuffed at them with the toe of his boot, but what could be wiped away already had been, and the rest had soaked in, darkening the wood.

He sniffed, certain that he could still smell the rank coppery odor of blood, the throat-catching scent of freshly butchered meat. And, of course, the other musky stench.

A skunk, no less.

What the hell did they mean by that? And who the hell would do such a thing anyway?

He stared at the ugly stain, wondering if it could be sanded away or whether he'd have to paint over it. One way or the other, it had to go. Made the customers nervous.

Made him a little nervous, too.

He glanced over his shoulder at the road, pushed open the heavy oak door and went inside, then locked the door behind him; the tavern didn't open till noon on Saturdays, and it was only half past eleven.

It was dark inside the bar—no windows to remind the customers of time passing them by—and he

waited for his eyes to adjust before crossing the room toward his office. He kept himself from looking at the chairs stacked on top of the tables, not wanting to notice anything out of place. It wasn't that he really expected any more surprises; the skunk episode just made him a little skittish.

The office had windows, narrow and long like in a bunker, but they admitted no light, hidden as they were behind heavy lined drapes. He was of an age when he did not wish to think of time passing *him* by either. He flicked the switch, his eyes searching the room, and then let out a sigh.

What was the world coming to, when a man could not go into his place of business without worrying about some nut-case coming after him?

Still, if anyone had it out for him, he was more than ready for them.

He kept the .44 magnum in the floor safe although it was a little inconvenient; to get to the gun, he had to kneel down, fool with the combination, and muscle open the reinforced-steel door. Not exactly a quick draw, but on those occasions when he drank more than he should—and with his temper—it was better that he have to work at getting the gun.

He'd have shot half the people in town by now if he kept it at hand.

It was a beauty, a Smith & Wesson, gun-metal blue like the cops used. The first time he'd shot it, he thought it was going to blow up in his hand. Damn, but it kicked, and made a noise like a small cannon, which he supposed it was.

Now he hefted the gun, enjoying the lethal weight of it, the solid, end-of-argument *feel* of it. Only a suicidal maniac would make a move against him with this kind of artillery in his hand.

Something thumped out in the bar, and he spun, even as his mind identified the noise as the ice maker dumping a batch of ice cubes.

"Jumping at shadows," he said aloud, and shook his head in disgust, lowering the gun. A fucking hair trigger. What had happened to his nerve?

A few years back it would have taken more than a dead skunk to get his attention. A few years back there had been nothing he wouldn't do, nothing that he was afraid of. A few years back . . .

Was that what this was all about?

He hid the gun in the drawer below the cash register and then practiced getting it out as quickly, and unobtrusively, as possible.

Finally, satisfied that he could arm himself at a moment's notice, he unlocked the doors.

Every time a customer came in, he looked up in anticipation, and he realized that, in a way, he wanted something to happen. He had never been adverse to a little action, as long as he knew that he'd come out on top.

The .44 guaranteed that.

Six

As she came out of the sheriff's office, Missy hesitated, frowning and squinting up at the sun. Another warm day, by the looks of it, the sky a baked, faded blue, with only those lacy-looking puffs of clouds which were hard put to provide even a moment's shade. The asphalt gave off waves of heat, reminding her of the summers when she was a child and the roads had softened, oozing tar which blackened the soles of her feet and resisted her mother's most determined scrubbings.

So long ago.

Missy sighed, pushed up the sleeves of her sweater, and started down the street toward the market; with her garden destroyed, she'd need store-bought vegetables to fix for supper. Waxy and tasteless, compared to her own, the flavor bred out much like common decency had been bred out of this generation of children.

Thirty-five years as a teacher had erased any illusions she once might have had about children. She had been high-spirited as a young girl, but nowadays they just ran wild. . . .

As the person who forced them to sit still and be quiet, who insisted on order and decorum, and who reported their misdeeds to their parents, she was often a target. In retaliation they soaped her windows, slashed her screens, and upended her garbage all over the lawn. But never before had they been so bold!

Her garden was sacred. It had always been the one place where her efforts were duly rewarded.

The little beasts . . . they would not get away with it this time, she would see to that. If the law was unable to protect her, she'd do it herself.

Ahead of her she noticed Charlotte Sinclair coming out of the bakery, hands full of white bags, her pudgy face fixed with the simpering smile which was meant to convey good humor, but which Missy secretly thought suggested indigestion or even an intestinal blockage.

"Missy!" Charlotte hurried in her direction, the simper replaced with a wide-eyed look which Missy recognized as concern; all of Charlotte's expressions had been copied, Missy was sure, from some nineteenth century tome on drama.

"Charlotte . . ."

"I heard about what happened, you poor dear." Charlotte rearranged the bakery bags to get a hand free and then patted Missy's arm. "You must have been terrified."

What she had been was mad as hell and she was tempted to say so, but Charlotte had a highly developed set of sensibilities and Missy wasn't up to

seeing the dramatic representation of shock. Instead she nodded and changed the subject.

"When did you get back from Europe?" Ever since Frank Sinclair died, his grieving widow had sought forgetfulness by traveling to all the places the two of them had planned to go when he retired from his law practice. Overinsured, Frank had provided the wherewithal for dozens of trips, and Charlotte had displayed a propensity for extravagance that must have set her cautious spouse spinning in his grave.

Charlotte dismissed Europe with a wave of her hand. "Last week." She wrinkled her nose. "There were so many tourists . . . it really wasn't much fun at all."

"No?" Imagine, Missy thought, finding tourists on a *tour!*

"Then again, I'm afraid I've gotten spoiled from the cruises. They're so much nicer than land tours, all that walking about. Of course, cruising is responsible for *this*." Charlotte held up the cluster of white bags and laughed, a high braying sound which ended in a snort. "I got so spoiled, every time you turn around, they're putting out food, I'd never seen so much food in my life. . . . . I just can't seem to exert any willpower."

"Hmm." Charlotte's willpower was, to Missy's mind, much talked about and seldom seen.

"You'll have to come over and see my vacation slides before they multiply . . . and I'm off again soon."

Missy grimaced. "Yes, well. I'd better be on my way now, there's so much for me to do at home."

"Oh dear, of course there must be!" Charlotte

leaned forward, mouth puckered, her lips primly brushing Missy's cheek. She smelled strongly of cinnamon. "Take care."

Missy cast a thankful glance heavenward as Charlotte bustled off. She resumed walking toward the market.

"I heard about what happened."

Missy looked up from the tomatoes. Lenore O'Hara stood across the vegetable bin, her hawkish eyes surveying the mounds of produce.

"Word gets around," Missy said.

"That it does, a small town like this."

Missy selected a tomato, sniffing at it; it might have been made of plastic for all the fragrance it gave off. She set it back down and picked up another.

"Maybe it was Mr. Goldstein."

"What?"

"Mr. Goldstein hates to lose business," Lenore said. "Maybe he did it."

Missy tried to imagine Horace Goldstein rampaging through the vegetable patch, his polished wing-tips kicking up tufts of greenery. That kind of exertion would certainly be contrary to his nature; the grocer was known for his sartorial splendor and there were those who whispered that he permed what remained of his hair.

Goldstein running amok was not at all likely, she thought, but she raised her eyebrows and pretended to consider the suggestion in deference to the woman's position. As secretary to the mayor, Lenore O'Hara reportedly had her finger on the town's

38

pulse, and little escaped her notice. In fact, over the years Lenore had become so entrenched in town politics that no one dared mention her rather questionable past.

Still, the notion of Horace trampling her garden was patently absurd, although it wouldn't do to say so. Instead she frowned. "No," she said after a moment, "I remember someone telling me that Horace has hay fever; if he'd done it, I would've heard him sneezing."

"Maybe so . . . but his son?"

The tone of Lenore's voice caught her attention and she looked closely at the woman's face. Unlike Charlotte, Lenore revealed little of her emotions; her features were composed and seemingly indifferent.

"What about his son?" Stephen had been in her fourth grade class, one of the few well-mannered children, but that had been before anyone knew about his trouble.

"I heard," Lenore said, "that they brought him back here to live."

"But surely he's—"

"The boy is sixteen now. I gather he was too much for that special *school* they had him in."

Missy didn't comment, but watched as Lenore's spidery fingers picked over the red onions.

"Of course, it's supposed to be a secret that he's home, shut up in that big old house all day . . ." Lenore glanced up and their eyes held. "Though in a little town like this, there aren't any real secrets, are there?"

39

Seven

Cody Austin roamed through the library aisles, stretching his legs, reading titles and stopping occasionally to leaf through the pages of a favorite book. Familiar passages he whispered, reverently, marveling, as always, in the power of often commonplace words.

Words were his opiate.

As a writer, he heard music in a finely crafted phrase, orchestrated into overture, melody, and refrain.

The essence of life, captured on the printed page. Thoughts, images, dreams . . . and nightmares. Glimpses into the dark recesses of place and time, or into the white light of imagination.

Yet fiction, as intoxicating as it could be, was only a pale reflection of the truth he found among the rows of nonfiction books. Those works held not the essence, but the whole cloth of life, in addition to perceptions of reality which defied the constraints of literary artifice.

The best of them seeking truth and finding it.

Capote's book, a masterpiece of research and

conjecture woven into a chilling story of murder. Reading it, he had a sense of the inevitable, of a force put in motion which could only end in tragedy.

Then there was the stunning power of Wambaugh's journey into the onion field. Even though he had read newspaper accounts of the same event, the book pulled him in, made him forget that he knew the outcome, and then shocked him back into awareness when the policeman was shot.

He'd read that passage over and over, and the last reading had as much impact as the first. He felt both betrayed at the loss of a well-liked character—a flesh-and-blood person who lived and breathed and then died on paper—and in awe of the author's talent, and it was the latter which compelled him to find a story of his own.

A murder of his own.

He had come upon the Tranquility murders by accident; his sister's monthly care package—she didn't think he ate well or often enough—arrived with newspapers cushioning the cookies from the jars of preserves.

At the bottom of the box was a paper which featured a recounting of the brutal, unsolved murders of Roger and Leigh Chandler Brown.

Looking at their photographs, along with one taken of their pretty dark-haired daughter being led away from the murder scene, and he'd known instantly that *this* was his story. This story would forever separate him from the ranks of novice journalists whose anonymous words were routinely

swallowed up by the media machine.

It had been slow going at first—a lot of years had passed and many of the principals had died—but he'd managed to uncover a few leads, and using skills acquired working summers for a private investigation agency, he had tracked them down.

Bit by bit, he put together the pieces of a story which had shattered under the weight of its deceit. All that was needed for it to come tumbling down was for him to cast a light into the shadowed, half-forgotten corners of the town's secrets.

Now, after months of intensive research, he was eager to get on with it.

The time had come to act.

At four he stood on the library stairs and took in a deep breath. It was still warm, although the sun was low in the sky, and he welcomed the breeze which dried the sweat on his brow.

Behind him the librarian jangled keys and he turned, surprised to catch her looking at him.

He smiled and nodded, but, eyes averted, she twisted the key forcefully in the lock, and then hurried off.

"Now what was that about?" he wondered aloud.

But there were other things to think about, and after a moment he started down the stairs.

Eight

"Don't tell me," Bucky Hightower said, raising his hands in mock surrender, "someone complained about the noise."

Noah surveyed the empty room and nodded. "I'll have to ask you to try to keep it down . . ." He slid onto a stool and tossed his hat on the bar.

"This business or do you want a drink?"

"I have a few questions."

"Then *I'll* have a drink." Bucky drew a draft beer and drank half of it, then looked at Noah expectantly. "So . . ."

"Who do you think did it?"

Bucky snorted. "I thought you were the one who's supposed to figure that out."

"Got any enemies?"

"Who hasn't?" He finished off the beer and peered thoughtfully into the mug. "You live long enough, you make enemies. You oughta know that."

Noah regarded him. "Thanks for the philosophy lesson, but I was looking for something a little more specific."

45

"You mean like someone who threatened to nail a skunk to my door? Sorry, can't help you there. . . . I've been living a life above reproach the past few years."

Noah knew better, but decided against saying so. "Maybe you tossed a drunk out of here for being rowdy, or lost your temper and cussed someone out . . ."

"Business being the way it is, I find myself a little more tolerant of human nature."

"Well," Noah said, "somebody out there is fixing to see how much harassment you're willing to take before you do something about it."

The sigh sounded as if it originated in Bucky's toes. "Hell, Sheriff, if I had a clue I'd tell you, but I don't and I can't. Like I said, I've been behaving myself. Maybe this was one of those 'isolated incidents' like they're always talking about on TV. Some crazy person, or maybe the ladies' temperance league is after my ass for running this joint."

Noah shook his head. "Whoever did it went to a lot of trouble. You got any idea how hard it is to catch a skunk? And then strangle it? Gut it?"

"What do you want from me? I said I don't know." Bucky moved away, back to the beer tap, and refilled his mug.

"I can't help you if you're not up front with me."

"Look . . . I'm not the only one in town who's been a target. Why don't you ask one of them?"

Noah studied Hightower's face, noting the sullen set of his mouth and the angry furrows across his broad forehead.

He'd get nothing out of this man. There were a lot of rumors going around, and if this was old trouble—which he suspected it might be—Bucky seemed determined to keep it private.

"All right," he said, reaching for his hat, "have it your way."

Nine

Paige slowed, turning into the gravel driveway, and then braked the Jaguar to a full stop. The house, nestled in a grove of pepper trees, was straight ahead. Paint graying, it seemed abandoned, desolate. . . .

For a moment she had an odd impression that she was looking into the past, like peering through a rain-beaded window, the colors diffuse, reality muted. Time had blurred around the edges and she almost expected to see herself, a child again, looking out an upstairs window.

This was home, despite the fact that she hadn't lived here for twenty-six years.

She eased the car forward.

The air smelled of acacia, and beyond the house she could see the yellow-flowered trees where they grew by the stream which ran along the south border of the property. So many times she had gathered great armfuls of blossoms from low-hanging branches, breathing in the sweet fragrance as she carried them home.

She smiled and started toward the porch, remembering how her mother, out of vases, had filled glasses and bottles and jars with sprigs of acacia.

It got to be a family joke; every spring her father teased her about leaving the trees bare, while her mother found more inventive ways to display the lemon-colored flowers. They had even floated clusters of them, like magnolia, in bowls filled with water.

The trees didn't bloom in December, but that spring, after her parents died, she had, once again, filled her arms. Throat aching, trying not to cry, she'd walked along the dirt road to the cemetery.

"I left some on the trees, Daddy," she'd whispered then, and for a few precious minutes, she'd felt near to them, a little less alone.

A week later she had returend to her grandmother's house in Southern California, and in a way, it was for the best, because there were no acacia trees to remind her.

But she had missed their subtle fragrance, she realized now. Maybe she would go down later. . . .

Something wasn't right.

She stopped, key in hand, and looked closely at the door. It was fractionally ajar and she reached out, pushing it open, watching as it swung inward.

"Aunt Ellen?"

She stepped just inside the threshold and listened but all was quiet. An unnatural quiet.

Someone was in the house.

The phone sat on a table in the hallway a few feet away, but she hesitated, unwilling to go farther into the room. Had the phone been connected yet? It would be safer, she thought, to go back to the car, but

as she turned she heard footsteps on the stairs.

"Hello?" A male voice. "Is someone there?"

Paige didn't answer.

The man who came into view a second later had a smile on his face. He stopped at the landing. Dark-haired, blue eyes without a hint of menace in them.

"Paige Brown?"

Their eyes held and she had a fleeting impression that she knew him from somewhere, had seen him before.

"Yes, and you're . . ."

"Cody Austin."

The name was vaguely familiar as well but she couldn't quite place it. A former patient?

"I wrote you . . ." he began, and took a step closer.

In spite of herself she moved backward.

". . . about an interview. For my book."

Austin, of course. The letter at work this morning. The one she'd torn up.

"You're almost impossible to reach," he said.

"On purpose." She made no effort to hide her annoyance. "I'm not interested, Mr. Austin, in talking to anyone about my family. I would think that should be fairly evident by now."

His smile held steady. "I was told as much by your attorney, who, by the way, does an excellent job of shielding you. He could give the CIA pointers in running a covert operation."

"But he didn't dissuade you . . ."

"No."

"What would it take to convince you that you're wasting your time?"

He shook his head. "I know what I'm doing. I'll

write the book anyway, with or without your help. I have to say, though, that I'm surprised that you're not more interested in finding out the truth about what happened."

"The truth?" She felt a rush of anger. "I'm not at all interested in your version of the truth, but maybe the sheriff would be. This *is* private property that you're trespassing on."

Maddeningly, the smile stayed put. "I'll go now, but I wonder if you're not the least bit curious about what I've managed to dig up."

"Some things are better left alone."

"I don't believe that, and I don't think you do either. You can't turn your back on it."

At the door he stopped, a foot away from her, and this time she saw something in his eyes, a look she recognized, having seen it in her own mirror. A look of anguish.

Neither of them spoke, and then he was gone.

Paige did not turn to watch after him.

Sundown came just as she carried the last of her luggage inside. The sky was full of color, soft pastels of gold and pink and blue, and she thought at once of the verse her father had taught her:

Red sky at night, a sailor's delight; red sky at morning, a sailor takes warning.

Take warning . . . somehow it had never seemed as ominous as it did now. She closed the door on the sunset and locked both locks.

52

Alone. Knowing how tired she would be after working all night and the long drive up, she had suggested to Aunt Ellen that they postpone her "homecoming" until tomorrow, but now, standing in the empty, silent house, she wished for company.

Shadows deepened in corners as she started up the stairs.

She was taking the master bedroom, since her own room was too small for the old-fashioned canopied bed she'd bought at an auction in Santa Barbara.

The movers had, without instruction, put it where her parents' bed had been.

She stood in the doorway and remembered the room as it had looked that night.

Her eyes filled with tears.

"I'm home," she said aloud.

Ten

He watched the house for a long time, waiting for the lights to go out.

Back pressed against a tree trunk, knees drawn up to his chest, he tried to ignore the night sounds. He told himself that there was nothing that could hurt him.

Not anymore . . . not since they'd taken the leather man away.

His stomach ached, reminding him that he hadn't eaten since morning, and then he had only had a banana and a few swallows of milk. He'd been hungry at lunch time, but he didn't want to go home, and there was nowhere else he could go.

He had no money to buy food, and the times he'd searched through the trash cans, he'd felt eyes watching him.

He did not like to eat in front of people.

"Like a hog in a trough," the man who pretended to be his father said.

As if he'd had a chance to learn better in the place they'd sent him.

No . . . he wouldn't think about that.

A muscle cramped in his left thigh and he rubbed it, but he didn't really mind the pain, not after all those shots and the pills which kept him from feeling anything. Anything except . . . a kind of burning.

When at last the house went dark, he got to his feet and cautiously made his way toward it. Because the place had been empty for so long—even before he was sent away—the yard was pitted with gopher holes. A careless step could result in a turned ankle.

Which would mean questions at home.

Actually, if he concentrated, he could make out the slightly darker patches of ground where the holes were.

"Whatever's this boy's problem, there's nothing wrong with his eyes."

The face that went with the voice came unbidden to his mind; watery blue eyes behind wire-rimmed glasses, fleshy lips that were always smacking, and a small, squashed-looking nose that didn't look like anyone could breathe through it.

He didn't remember the doctor's name, but he remembered what everyone called him: the Guzzler.

The Guzzler had stood up for him.

"He doesn't belong here. Take him home."

"Listen, Doctor, I pay good—"

"That isn't my concern. Your son doesn't belong in a place like this."

"But the other doctors told me . . ."

He put his hands over his ears and pressed hard,

trying to shut out the voices. A rumbling sound filled his head and he closed his eyes, imagining that the earth would open up beneath his feet and take him in.

Somewhere safe.

Somewhere they couldn't get at him.

Eleven

Paige had counted on exhaustion to help her fall asleep the first night home, but as tired as she felt, she was wide awake an hour after going to bed. Arms and legs heavy with fatigue, she lay motionless, eyes open to the darkness, and tried to will herself to sleep.

Like so many other nights, her thoughts worked against her. A kaleidoscope of ever-changing images crowded her mind, a montage of past and present slipping in and out of focus. Faces fractured into their component parts, the eyes haunting her. . . .

Alex, who had a passion for computers, would call it a case of too much input. Overloaded circuits.

An excess of memory.

Alex . . . bless his analytical heart.

Her life would be simpler if only she could love him, but the feelings weren't there and she didn't think they ever would be. She'd told him as much, but he maintained that love was "learned behavior," and he was more than willing to teach her what she needed to know.

But for her, there had to be more; there had to be heat.

Who had said that love was Nature's second sun? Balanced on the edge of sleep, she let her mind wander. . . .

She hurried through the house, going from window to window, trying to get a clear look at a man—was it a man?—who ran toward the trees.

Someone had to stop him.

She had to stop him.

But when she turned, he was there, reaching for her with bloodied hands.

She opened her mouth to scream. . . .

Paige sat upright, feeling the cold rush of adrenaline as it flooded into her veins. Flinging back the covers, she was on her feet before she realized that it had been a dream.

No one was after her.

Outside the wind rustled through the pepper trees.

SUNDAY

Twelve

Bucky cautiously sniffed the air, half expecting to detect the musky aroma of skunk juice, but the night breezes had cleared even the most determined odors. He couldn't smell a thing.

Good enough. After breathing beer fumes all evening, the last thing he needed was a dose of that particular aerosol.

He checked the tavern door a final time and then turned to walk stiffly down the steps, feeling the ache in his calves after so many hours on his feet.

It had been a long night.

Business had picked up around eight, peaked near midnight, and at closing he'd had to usher a somewhat weepy Otis Carter out the door and into the red Caddy that was all Otis had left after his wife's lawyer was through with him.

That had been over an hour ago.

Now, by the looks of things, he was the only person still up and about.

The good people of Tranquility were asleep in their beds. Safe. Snug. Cozy.

"Heartwarming," he said, and laughed.

The sound carried.

Gliding down the road, the car straddling the line, Bucky blinked and yawned, then cracked a window.

Fresh air stung his face and made his eyes water, but it was better than dozing off only to wake up dead.

Wake up dead. That had been one of Naomi's little sayings, as in: "Hit me one more time, bastard, and you're gonna wake up dead one morning."

A class act, that Naomi.

Bucky tightened his grip on the steering wheel. The problem with Naomi, to his way of thinking, was that he hadn't hit her hard or often enough.

A pretty woman, when he'd met her, a sloe-eyed blonde, a shade over five feet tall with a die-for-it body. Her only flaw was her voice. A: she sounded like a drag queen on speed, and B: she always had something to say.

Still, he should have suspected right off the bat that something wasn't kosher: what did a female who looked like that want with him? His buddies always joked that his picture was in the dictionary, as illustration of the word "ugly."

It had to be money.

He owned a business and had a little put back in a few scattered accounts. Not rich, but better than comfortable. More than adequate for little Naomi.

And for him? He'd never been lucky with women, and he had no hesitation in paying for anything as long as he got value returned.

Being an old-fashioned kind of guy, he'd married her.

Before long, her voice began to get to him. He tried to ignore her, but it was like trying to ignore a dentist's drill. In fact, listening to her made his teeth hurt.

So he'd hit her.

And when, crying, nose running, her face streaked with mascara, she'd whine that he couldn't treat her that way, he'd hit her a little harder.

She never did learn.

Then she started with the "wake up dead" threats.

He was well rid of her, although once in a while—not as often lately—he thought about that hot little body and had a few regrets.

The headlights illuminated the driveway and he noticed that the shrubs were overgrown, extending spiny fingers into the narrow lane. That would have to be tended to before his paint job was ruined.

Mind on that, he didn't notice right away that the house was dark. Didn't notice it, in fact, until he switched off the headlights and found himself unable to see.

Had he forgotten to leave the porch light on?

"Damn." Annoyed, he flung open the car door. The interior light, dim as it was, blinded him further, and he lunged out into the blur of black and gray shapes.

A scurrying sound came from his left and then a blow struck him above his left ear.

He swung his arms around him, but nothing was

within reach, and he fell to his knees.

A second blow to the base of his neck sent him sprawling, face first, and he had a mouth full of dirt and rock. He gagged and choked and tried to take a breath of air . . .

And couldn't. . . .

Thirteen

Ellen cracked an egg into the skillet and tried to ignore the nausea that looking at it provoked.

She'd woken twice during the night, feeling ill, and both times had hurried to the bathroom only to kneel helplessly on the cold floor, unable to bring anything up. Her abdominal muscles were sore from trying.

A scrambled egg on toast had seemed bland enough to soothe a queasy stomach, but watching it cook was making her sick again. The egg white, semicooked, appeared viscous and somehow vile. She swallowed hard, and then lifted the skillet off the burner, shoving it to one side of the stove.

Later. She would eat later. She sat down at the table and took a tentative sip of tea.

Luckily Martin had never been one for breakfasts.

She could hear him moving about upstairs, the sounds, like him, quiet and purposeful. He was, she estimated, midway through his Sunday morning routine.

Perhaps another five minutes before he came down.

Ellen slipped her hand into the pocket of her bathrobe and closed her fingers around the small plastic vial.

Just having it in her hand made her feel a little better.

Overhead, the footsteps faded as Martin left the bedroom and started down the hall. He would stop in the den to look through the Saturday mail. . . .

She twisted the cap off the bottle even as she brought it from her pocket. Spilling the tablets into her palm, she took two of them, and noted that there were only half a dozen left. She'd have to get more. She placed the pills on the tip of her tongue and washed them down with a swallow of lukewarm tea.

She began to feel better a few moments later.

Ellen could feel Martin's eyes following her as she refilled the kettle and took it to the stove. Keeping her hands from shaking was a major effort, even with the calming effects of the medication taking hold.

"Are you sure you're up to this?"

Ellen did not answer immediately, centering the kettle on the burner before turning to face him with a smile.

"You worry too much," she said. "I'm fine." She felt a shiver of distaste at repeating her litany of health.

"You were up last night."

That surprised her; as long as they'd been married, she'd never known Martin to wake at night. There had been a time last fall, after she'd been released

from the hospital, when his deep sleep had troubled her. She feared that she might have an attack and be unable to wake him. . . .

Now she nodded. "But I'm better this morning."

"Paige would understand, you know. She's a doctor, she knows how important it is that you don't overdo."

Ellen tucked her hands into her pockets, one hand gripping the bottle, and smiled determinedly. He mustn't see that he'd upset her. "Well," she said mildly, "it's important to me that we welcome her home, to her *real* home, after all this time. It's the least we can do."

Martin's expression was unreadable.

Behind her the kettle began to whistle.

"I wonder," he said a few minutes later, "whether Patrice Chandler did the right thing, leaving that house to Paige."

Ellen looked at her husband. "What do you mean?"

He did not raise his eyes from the newspaper. "I would've torn it down, if it had been mine."

She didn't understand. "Tear down the house?" Her words were slow coming from her mouth and she frowned, hoping that he wouldn't notice, but she wasn't overly concerned. The pills kept her from being too concerned about anything. Anything at all.

"I can't imagine anyone wanting to live there." He turned the page. "And it can't have been money . . .'"

69

"What?"

"If Mrs. Chandler was concerned about the loss, from tearing the building down, she wouldn't have let the house set empty all those years."

"Empty . . ." The words echoed in her mind, chased by a half-formed thought that evaporated when she tried to take a closer look at it.

"But I guess if you're rich enough, you can afford a shrine or two."

Ellen shook her head, ready to protest; her brother's house, after all, he was talking about her brother. . . .

Martin got up from the table. "I wonder if the old lady wasn't a little senile, there at the end . . ." He patted her hand and then turned away. "I would've torn it down."

He was gone before she had formulated a safe argument, something that she could say and still keep them away from those things they could never discuss.

She sighed and took a sip of tea.

As she began preparations for the homecoming dinner, she heard the siren.

She stopped what she was doing to listen to the thin wail which rose and fell as the sound was deflected by canyon walls and thick groves of trees.

Sirens weren't common in Tranquility, but they always had fascinated her, and she had learned, through the years, to track them through the labyrinth of dirt roads which twisted through town.

70

She went to the back door and opened it, stepping out on the porch so that she could hear better. In her present state, it took her a few minutes to pin it down.

This one was headed toward Oak Ridge.

She went back inside; no one she cared for lived on Oak Ridge Road.

Fourteen

The drive was blocked when Noah arrived, the town's four patrol cars positioned at angles to keep the curious out and, by the look of it, the ambulance in.

From what he'd heard on the way over, there was no need for the ambulance. The coroner's van hadn't arrived yet.

Joseph Ramos, the deputy standing at point, his face a little pale, nodded as Noah came up to the perimeter.

"Dead?"

Joe grimaced. "Very."

That he'd heard as well. And inferred as much from the shocked, guarded voices on the radio.

But he wasn't prepared for how very dead Bucky Hightower proved to be.

The body was nailed to the front door.

Noah stepped over the yellow crime scene marker and came up behind the photographer, a baby-faced youth who looked like he should be taking pictures of little kids on Shetland ponies.

"Kevin . . ." He squatted to one side, out of the

way, and studied the rusted nails—railroad spikes?—
which had been hammered through the dead man's
palms.

"Nice, huh?"

Noah shook his head. "Somebody didn't like
him."

Camera flashes lit Hightower's bloodied face, but
the eyes had dulled and would never blink again.

"Somebody," Kevin said, lowering the Pentax, "is
crazy."

Looking at the third piece of metal, a good two feet
long, which entered Bucky's mouth and pinned his
head to the door, Noah was inclined to agree.

Fifteen

The telephone rang as Felicity sat down to breakfast and she held her breath as her mother answered, praying for a wrong number. . . .

"Yes," her mother said, "yes, I heard about it, never mind how."

Felicity had no desire to listen to her mother's phone conversations, but given the claustrophobic closeness of the kitchen, there was no way to avoid it. She couldn't leave the room until she had eaten, and the only alternative was to put her hands over her ears, something she had done once before, when the subject of discussion had been the unlikelihood of her ever marrying.

For that transgression, she'd endured a week of goading.

"Can't stand the truth?" Lenore O'Hara had taunted. "My, aren't we sensitive!"

This morning, at least, they apparently weren't talking about her.

Small favors, she thought.

"Had it coming to him," her mother said, voice strident and righteous.

Felicity looked down at her pancakes, which she'd buttered and sprinkled with sugar—her favorite topping—and realized she was no longer hungry.

"It'll take some solving," Lenore went on, "with so many people glad to see the son of a bitch dead. . . . I'm just surprised it didn't happen years ago . . ."

A careful sideways glance allowed Felicity to see her mother's face, whose lips, as always, were drawn in a tight, grim line.

The bright sunlight that streamed through the kitchen window accentuated a patchwork of tiny wrinkles around the older woman's eyes and mouth, and Felicity wondered how many of those wrinkles had come from sour looks and from taking satisfaction at someone else's trouble.

Like now.

Who had died, she wondered, and then looked away, unable to stand the expression of—was it gratification?—on her mother's face.

"Well, I have my suspicions . . . but I'll keep 'em to myself until I see how things develop."

Her mother's laugh grated on her nerves and she looked down at her plate, wondering if she could make herself eat. She cut the pancakes into tiny wedges and then pushed them around her plate. She took a sip of orange juice.

"No, I'd just rather not let everyone know that I'm keeping track. . . . Some folks in this town would get a little nervous if they had a notion . . ."

Felicity knew immediately what her mother was referring to: the journals.

*　　　*　　　*

She had come across them years ago, on a day she'd stayed home from school with a stubborn fever.

Alone in the house, not really ill enough to stay in bed, she wandered around, looking aimlessly into drawers and cupboards for something to relieve the boredom that had begun as soon as the novelty of being home wore off.

After a while, goose bumps rising in delicious anticipation, she'd gone into her mother's darkened bedroom, and closed the door carefully behind her.

The room was silent in a way that her own room never was, and she wondered if just being strange to a place could bring about that special quiet.

At first she only looked, standing at the vanity, eyes wide with wonder at the array of bottles and jars that crowded the tabletop. She knew better than to touch them; if anything were out of place, her mother would somehow know.

Felicity peeked in the closet and, unable to resist the temptation a moment longer, slipped her bare feet into a pair of red satin high-heeled shoes. She had never seen her mother wear them, but they were beautiful. . . .

If *she* had a pair of red shoes, she would wear them every day.

The click of the heels as she walked back and forth across the wood floor made her feel very grown up. She went to stand in front of the mirror, and admired the look of red satin against her pale skin.

When her ankles tired, she wobbled over to the bed and sat down.

She found the journals—there were five of them—in her mother's bedside table.

They had gray covers with red bindings, and the

word "journal" was printed across the front of each one in gold letters. Each of the books was filled with her mother's handwriting. There was not a blank page or empty line in any of the books.

She read a little, here and there, and decided that these were storybooks her mother had written, only these stories were about real people instead of princes and princesses.

There were words she didn't understand, and a few names she'd never heard, but one thing became clear: there were no happy endings.

All the people in her mother's stories were very, very bad.

Felicity hadn't thought about the journals in a long time.

Now she wondered if her mother still kept them in the same place.

Sixteen

Paige opened her eyes, uncertain, for a moment, of where she was as the last vestiges of the dream faded away.

She had dreamt of the girl, the ten-year-old child she'd pronounced dead the morning before, who, in the dream, stood at the end of a long, empty hall, beckoning her with a gentle smile.

Fingers of sunlight poked through the folds of the drapes and streaked across the darkened room. She watched as dust particles swirled hypnotically within the golden rays, an image that evoked memories from childhood which were so vivid that she expected, when she raised her hand, for it to be a child's hand reaching toward the light.

The memory, like the dream before it, gave way to awareness.

It was morning, and she was home.

She slipped from beneath the covers and went to the window to let the daylight in. The sun warmed

her as she looked out on the morning.

Her grandmother had promised her that one day she would be able to come back to the house.

"It won't be the same, child, don't think that it will. But I'll keep it for you, for you to do what you want, when you're old enough to decide."

Patrice Chandler had been right; it wasn't the same. The yard she remembered as lush and green and endless seemed barren now, the remaining patches of grass turned brown by the sun.

Her swing, which her father had put up when she was five, was broken and now hung by a single length of rusted chain. She could still recall standing beneath the tree, looking up, breathless with excitement, as she watched him fastening the thick loops of that chain—which she'd thought was strong enough to last forever—around a sturdy branch.

Paige smiled. In her mind she could hear the jingle of the metal links as she swung, pumping her legs to go higher, higher. She could feel the air lift her hair off her neck and the odd sensation in the pit of her stomach as the swing reached its apex and the momentum suddenly changed.

Falling back, even with Father waiting behind her, frightened her; she was never certain that she would not just plummet to the ground.

Yet even with the fear, the exhilaration of the upward swing proved irresistible.

Risks, she'd learned at an early age, were sometimes worth taking.

*   *   *

She saw the large manila envelope when she reached the turn in the stairway.

It had apparently been shoved under the door and now lay in the middle of the entryway, an unwelcome intrusion into her morning.

Mr. Austin hadn't given up, then.

Had she really expected him to? Did any journalist ever give up on a story?

Paige continued down the stairs, tempted to ignore whatever message the envelope held, but as she crossed the hall, she hesitated and then stopped. What harm was there in looking?

She picked up the envelope, which she noted was sealed with a wide strip of reinforced tape; there was no writing on either side of it.

Cody Austin knew something about intrigue, she thought. In spite of herself, she was curious.

In the kitchen she found a knife and slit the envelope open, then pulled out a plain white folder, which was also secured with tape.

As she looked at the folder, she was suddenly overwhelmed by a feeling of dread.

Even so, she held the blade of the knife steady as it cut through the tape.

She put the knife down before opening the folder.

Photographs.

Three black-and-white photographs, taken, years ago, in the room where she now stood.

The bodies had been removed and only the stains on the floor remained.

Paige stared at the photos, torn between revulsion and fascination. As a child, she had been kept from

reading about the murder of her parents, and only in her imagination had she "seen" the aftermath of that violence.

The dark stains were more awful than anything she had imagined.

They were real.

Seventeen

It took a while to unpin Bucky Hightower's head from the door.

Noah stood aside, watching as Hoskins, the medical examiner from the county seat, worked at prying the metal rod out of the wood. He tried not to wince at the sound of it.

"Maybe we could cut through the door," someone suggested, "and remove the entire section, to preserve the crime scene."

The ME looked up. "Crime scene be damned! You've got your prints and pictures and measurements. . . . I suppose you'd want him buried with this . . . this *lance* through his head."

"This is a murder," Noah reminded him, "he didn't just get clumsy eating shish kebab."

Hoskins glared. "What this is, is a human being." Then he frowned and sighed, and when he went on, the anger was gone from his voice. "There's no evidence being destroyed by pulling him free."

Noah nodded. "You're right. Everyone's a little shook about this, and we're trying to go by the book . . ."

"The book," the man echoed.

"I know." Noah looked at the clotted blood which filled Hightower's gaping mouth. "Imposing order on disorder . . . but it's often not as futile as it seems."

The zipper of the body bag jammed at midpoint and resisted their efforts to unstick it. The thick stench of blood and postmortem bodily fluids was enough to deter further attempts.

Bucky's ruined face reproached them as they loaded him into the coroner's van. The doors were shut and locked.

"Will you be down for the autopsy?" Hoskins wiped his hands on a bloodied towel.

"What time?"

The ME peered at his watch and then began to rub at the face of it with a towel. "It's eleven now . . . say three o'clock."

"I'll be there," Noah said.

"By the way, Sheriff, there's something I can tell you before the autopsy . . ."

"Yes?"

"He was alive when that thing was pounded through him. Unconscious, perhaps, but alive."

After the van pulled away, Noah turned his attention to the collection of evidence.

They had found a .44 magnum beneath the driver's seat of Hightower's car.

The car itself, which had already been photographed and dusted for prints, was being impounded. The doors were sealed, and a tow truck had arrived to take it down to the crime lab. There technicians

would vacuum the interior to collect any materials—hair, fibers, dirt—which might be related to the crime.

It was possible, although not likely, that the killer had been driven to the scene in the victim's car. If that had been the case, why had Hightower not used the means of self-defense he'd brought along? Unless . . .

Noah frowned. Too early, he thought, to speculate on a suspect.

He divided the crime scene into roughly equal quadrants and assigned a deputy to each.

"I want you to concentrate on searching for any indications of a struggle—trampled grass, scuff marks in the dirt, drops of blood—or any signs that might indicate in which direction Hightower's attacker fled. Something as simple as a piece of fabric snagged on a bush might prove to be the link between a suspect and the crime scene. We can't afford to overlook anything."

"Do you have any suspects in mind?" Joe Ramos looked decidedly better, Noah observed, now that the body had been removed.

Noah shook his head. "Not yet. Our best bet, at this stage, is to collect any and all evidence that the laboratory may be able to use to identify a perpetrator. For now, we need to keep our eyes and minds open. Let's get to work."

Noah used Bucky's key to get into the house through the back door. He walked through the silent

85

rooms, careful not to disturb anything.

He was almost certain that Hightower had been attacked and killed outside, but procedure required that he examine all alternatives. It would not do for him to focus single-mindedly on a presumption and neglect other possibilities.

The deceased had not been much of a housekeeper. The house smelled like stale smoke and dirty dishwater.

Dust dulled the surfaces of tables and shelves, and coated the inside of the windows. Clothes were draped over the backs of chairs, and magazines were strewn across the floor in front of the couch. A bottle with an inch of clear liquid left in it acted as a place mark for Miss November.

"Shit, Bucky," he said, "I thought you only read the articles."

There were none of the telltale signs of violence in any of the rooms. No blood, nothing broken, no ransacking as might be expected if a burglary were interrupted. All the windows were locked, and the dirt on the windowsills was undisturbed.

The house, for all of its clutter, did not look like a place where someone had been killed.

More than that was the *feel* of it, the very stillness of the air; there was no lingering sense of rage. Bucky Hightower had not been attacked in these rooms.

Whatever had happened, happened outside under the cover of darkness.

Eighteen

Horace Goldstein looked up from his sandwich as his son came into the kitchen. The boy was dressed, as usual, in jeans, a dark colored, long-sleeved flannel shirt, and moccasins. The golden hair that everyone had made such a fuss over years ago was tangled and dirty.

"Where you been all night?"

Stephen stopped dead in his tracks and lowered his eyes.

Horace felt a flash of anger. Avoidance . . . the same tactic that Susanna had always used. The boy had learned his lessons well: the down-turned eyes, the quivering mouth, the slight color rising across the high cheekbones that he'd also inherited from her. Coming from the boy, however, the effect was of cowardice, pure and simple.

"I'm talking to you," he said.

Stephen shifted his feet.

"Do you hear me?"

A barely perceptible nod.

"So . . . where were you?" Horace took a bite of the sandwich and chewed, eyes watering from the onion, while he waited for an answer. He sniffed and wiped at his face with a napkin.

"I was out in the woods."

"All night?" He studied the boy and frowned. "Haven't you come to enough grief wandering around out there?"

Stephen's features went blank, as if the muscles in his face had suddenly atrophied. It was a look Horace was familiar with, a look that turned back his questions and filled him with disgust.

The look of a cretin.

Horace flung his half-eaten sandwich on the plate. "Go to your room, God damn you."

Moving almost sideways, the boy shuffled away.

He would lock him in tonight. When the doctors had insisted that he bring Stephen home, he had first installed locks on all the inside doors and wrought iron bars on the windows.

Punishment was the only thing that his son understood.

He stopped in front of the mantel and peered at the pictures of his wife.

Who would have guessed, looking at Susanna's angelic face, that she would give birth to a less than perfect child? It was genetic, he supposed, the result of years of inbreeding common to the Kentucky hills where she'd been born.

But she *was* beautiful, a delicate, fair-skinned

creature unlike any of the girls of his youth. Pale blue eyes, hair the color of corn silk, she was the dream he'd been afraid to dream.

Only later did he discover the flaws behind the mask.

And by then . . . it had been too late.

Nineteen

"You shouldn't have gone to all this trouble," Paige said, drawing her fingers across the pressed linen tablecloth.

The table was beautifully set with her aunt's best china, silver, and crystal, and distinguished by a centerpiece of orchids. A decanter of red wine captured a ray of sunlight and cast ruby-colored sparkles throughout the dining room.

Paige turned and took Ellen's hands in hers.

"Thank you."

Ellen's smile deepened. "I was glad to do it. It's . . . it's nice to have you home."

"And nice to *be* home. I can't tell you how much I looked forward to this. Now, is there anything I can do to help?" For a second, she thought she saw a flicker of anxiety cross her aunt's face, but then it was gone.

"No, dear, everything's done in the kitchen. . . . All we have to do is wait for your uncle to get home, so we can eat."

"Where is Uncle Martin?"

"Oh . . . he got a call, I suppose," Ellen said, "I

91

really don't know."

"The life of a country doctor."

"Yes, that. But he'll be home soon . . ." Her face brightened. "Why don't we have a glass of wine while we're waiting?"

"I'd like that."

"Good."

Paige watched Ellen hurry to the table. There was something in her aunt's manner that reminded her of a child's glee at doing the forbidden.

But why should that be?

They took their drinks outside and sat in the shade by the pool. A breeze fluttered the canopy above them, the only sound to break the calm.

"It's so peaceful here."

Ellen stroked the stem of the wine glass. "That's why we stayed, after . . ." She blinked and frowned. "Martin thought it was best. It was difficult, for a while, being here. I kept expecting to see Roger walking down the street . . ."

"I know," Paige said softly, "I find myself listening for my father's footsteps, and my mother's voice, calling me to dinner."

There was fresh pain in Ellen's eyes. "How much worse for you . . . being in that house."

"It's where I want to be." She tasted the wine, keeping it in her mouth for a moment before swallowing, and then looked at her aunt.

"Of course, that's your decision, but . . ." Ellen hesitated.

"Go on."

Ellen averted her eyes. "I would be . . . fright-ened . . . to stay alone in that house."

"Frightened of what?"

A tremulous smile. "So many things."

Paige watched as her aunt finished the wine and nervously licked her lips.

"Is there something wrong?"

The sound of a car intruded upon the stillness.

"Come," Ellen said, getting to her feet and extending a hand to Paige. "Martin's home."

"They're saying in town that he still may have been alive when the stakes were driven in," Martin said, piling potatoes on his plate. "Of course, he woundn't have been alive for long afterward. . . . I imagine it severed the spine."

"Oh Martin . . . not while we're eating."

He ladled gravy over slices of turkey and the potatoes. "Paige is a doctor, she's used to this kind of thing, aren't you, Paige?"

"I don't know that I'd say 'used to'; 'resigned to' might be a more accurate phrase."

"But not at supper."

There was an undertone of sharpness in her aunt's voice that caught Paige by surprise, and she looked up in time to see them exchange an oddly formal glance.

"As you wish."

They lapsed into silence. For several minutes the clatter of cutlery was the only noise in the room.

*   *   *

After supper, Ellen went upstairs to rest.

Martin poured brandy into Paige's glass, then into his own, and sat opposite her.

"I hope Aunt Ellen didn't tire herself . . ."

Her uncle shook his head. "She didn't sleep well last night, and . . . she may have had too much wine."

"How is she?"

"Stubborn." His smile was rueful. "Her cardiologist tells me she's her own worst enemy."

"That's probably true about most of us."

"Agreed. But you'd think, being married to a doctor, that she'd be a little more compliant."

Paige regarded her uncle thoughtfully. "I'm surprised at that. When I talked to her, after she got out of the hospital, I thought she was very concerned, and was making every effort to follow doctor's orders.

"Yes, at first. Less so now."

"Why? What changed?"

Martin swirled the brandy in his glass. "I haven't talked to her about it . . . she *won't* talk about it . . . but I gather she's distanced herself from it. None of it's real to her."

"Is there anything I can do?"

Again he shook his head. "I wish I could tell you, but I hardly know what to do myself."

Aunt Ellen was still resting when Paige left, a little after five.

Twenty

Noah had learned, over the years, to keep his distance from the autopsy table, and now he stood far enough back to avoid the bits of flesh and bone that might be flung by the saw. The ozone odor of electricity intermingling with the smell of organic decay assaulted his nostrils, and by proxy, his gut.

"Can you see from there?" Hoskins asked, not looking up.

"As much as I want to."

Hoskins laughed, a short, hard sound that echoed off the green-tiled walls. "A little faint of heart?"

Noah refused to be goaded; every medical examiner he had ever known seemed to take a perverse pleasure in sharing the more grisly aspects of the postmortem. "Look at this," the ME would say with glee, and hold up a bloodied handful of gore as if it were the holy grail.

Hoskins slipped some gleaming thing into the scale which was suspended above the table. "Liver . . . weighs twelve hundred, say twelve hundred and forty grams. Capsule is intact and . . . the parenchyma is firm and is . . . homogeneous."

"That's good to know," Noah said under his breath.

"What?"

"Nothing." He leaned against a second, and empty, table, feeling the cold metal through his shirt. "How much longer is this gonna take?"

Hoskins reached back into the abdominal cavity, his brow furrowed with concentration. "Why? Getting hungry?"

He forced a smile and shook his head. "Just got a lot to do and not much time to do it in."

There was a wet, sucking sound, and Hoskins pulled a loop of intestine from the body and peered beneath it. "Well, Mr. Hightower and I are in no hurry. This is his last chance to tell us what happened to him, and I, for one, am going to listen."

"Right," Noah said.

It went on.

Noah waited in the outer office for Hoskins to finish cleaning up.

It was now after five; the autopsy had taken more than two hours and had been one of the most thorough postmortem examinations he'd ever witnessed. Hoskins certainly knew his stuff.

Now, maybe, he'd get some answers.

The door opened and Hoskins came in, dressed again in street clothes, looking none the worse for having spent the afternoon up to his elbows in a corpse. He went in a straight line to the coffee pot.

"A little caffeine, Sheriff?" He poured what looked

like black syrup into a cup.

"No thanks."

"A cigarette, then?"

"No."

He looked at Noah, apparently amused. "What, no vices? You're not going to be an interesting case if you don't start abusing your body."

"I leave that to other people."

Hoskins laughed. "I'll bet you do." He sat at the desk, put his feet up, and lit a cigarette, taking a deep draw. He exhaled in a sigh. "So . . ."

"Tell me."

"About the last, fated hours of our friend, Mr. Hightower?"

Noah waited.

"Hmm. All right. Cause of death." He blew a cloud of smoke toward the ceiling. "A toss-up, really. The—I'll call it the weapon, for want of a better word—the weapon was driven through the soft tissues of the posterior wall of the pharynx . . . the back of the mouth . . . with great force."

"How great?"

"It would be difficult to measure, but I'd imagine that only an adult male would have the upper body strength that would be . . . necessary."

"Go on."

"The weapon shattered the first cervical vertebra—the atlas, as it is sometimes called—and nearly transected the spinal cord. That would cause immediate paralysis, most significantly of the respiratory system."

"Meaning he couldn't breathe."

Hoskins inclined his head. "A fatal injury in itself . . . further complicated by the copious amounts of blood which filled his lungs. You could say it was a race, as to which problem would kill him first. . . . He either suffocated from respiratory paralysis, or drowned in his own blood. The weapon was, you might say, a double-edged sword."

"I see. What about his other wounds?"

"The puncture wounds through the palmar region of his hands were made while he was still alive. He also sustained several blows to the head . . . there are contusions of the scalp, above the left ear and in the occipital area, but the skull was not fractured. There were several superficial cuts inside his mouth and I extracted a few small pieces of gravel. Not a pleasant death by any means."

"Would they . . . would the blows to the head have been enough to knock him out?"

"Probably."

"Just probably?"

"It may have only stunned him . . . incapacitated him long enough for his attacker to . . . hammer him to the door. You know that blood stops flowing after the heart stops beating?"

"Yes?"

"Based on the amount of blood at the scene, I would say that, regardless of whether he was knocked out or not, enough time passed between the infliction of the first wounds and the last . . . for Hightower to have regained consciousness before he was killed. He may have looked into his killer's eyes while . . . while it was being done to him." Hoskins stubbed out his

cigarette and immediately lit another.

Noah grimaced "Jesus!"

"A *very* unpleasant death," the medical examiner repeated. "I wonder . . . he must have had a chance to cry out . . . I wonder why no one heard him scream."

Noah had been wondering the same thing.

Twenty-one

Paige saw it as soon as she opened the door: a manila envelope, similar to the one she had found earlier. It lay in the center of the hallway like a blemish on the dark wood floor. It was thicker than the first, but looked to be sealed in the same manner.

"Damn him," she whispered.

She turned quickly and shut the door, turning the dead bolt with a savage twist.

"Damn him!"

Leaving the envelope where it lay, she went through the house, checking the windows and doors, finding everything locked and in order.

He had not, then, been in the house, nor had he broken the law.

Knowing that did not decrease her sense of violation; she made a second tour of the rooms, closing blinds and drapes, shutting out the twilight . . . and prying eyes.

By the time she finished, her anger had abated. She did not have to open Austin's little communique, and she would not. It was nothing more than aggressively delivered junk mail.

She threw it in the trash.

The bath water was warm and scented and she lay back in the tub, eyes closed, letting it soothe her.

Los Angeles seemed very far away.

As she'd intended it to be. The time was coming when she would have to make a decision: her two-year contract with Southern California Emergency Physicians was up for renewal on July 1, and she needed to do a lot of soul-searching before she signed another.

Lately she'd had doubts about the way her life was going, and her work was a big part of it. Six years in practice as an ER physician and she was, in the vernacular so popular with social scientists, burned out.

Alex said she worked too hard.

It was all she knew to do. Getting through college, medical school, an internship, and residency had been the focus of her life from the moment she'd decided to become a doctor. There had been time for little else.

She'd thought she needed nothing else.

She'd thought that a medical practice would fill all the empty places.

It hadn't.

"You've lost so much, Paige, that I wonder if it can ever be made up," her grandmother had said, her voice breathless from the effort to speak, on the day before she died.

"Don't worry about me."

"So much at such an early age . . ."

"Hush, Gran, you'll tire yourself."

Gran's voice fading: *"You were robbed . . . they took everything . . . they took it all . . ."*

Paige leaned forward and turned the hot water on, then settled back, feeling the water lap at her, welcoming the currents of heat which eddied around her legs. Steam swirled off the surface of the water.

"Cry for me, Gran," she said, closing her eyes. "I have no tears left."

She slid between the cool sheets and shivered at the feel of them against her bare skin. She burrowed deeper beneath the covers, pulling them up around her neck, and in a moment she began to feel warm again.

It was early still, but the bath had relaxed her and she hoped that she would be able to get to sleep.

If she tried not to think . . .

Just to sleep . . .

Warm hands stroked her, touched her, caressed her, and she gave herself over to the sensation, moving closer to the heat of the body next to hers.

She heard his breath in her ear, felt it on her neck, and she turned her face to him, seeking the taste of his mouth, the pressure of his lips. His kiss pleasured her in a way she'd not thought possible, and she entwined her fingers in his hair, holding him to her.

She ached with wanting, and she moved closer, unable to think of anything but the sweet relief he could offer.

"Oh," she breathed, taking the weight of his body, feeling the searing heat of his skin. . . .

There was just enough light to see his face as he moved above her.

Paige woke with a start, her pulse racing. She was drenched with sweat. She threw off the covers and sat up, letting the air cool her.

Her rational mind argued that the combination of a too-warm bath and thick blankets had induced a feverish dream, into which Cody Austin had intruded.

It didn't mean anything.

She got out of bed and went to the bureau to get a nightgown. It clung to her, held to her body by the dampness of her skin, but she was no longer comfortable with her nakedness.

Unable to go back to sleep, she went downstairs. After a moment's hesitation, she retrieved the manila envelope from the trash.

Twenty-two

The photographs covered the coffee table.

He stared at them, his eyes moving from one to the next, the shock he'd felt when he'd first seen them, months ago, now dulled to dismay. There was something about the black-and-white images that became less real the more he studied them. That sense of unreality provided the necessary distance, he thought, to ensure that he remained objective.

Had she opened the envelope yet? If so . . . how did she feel? Neither objective nor distant, unless she were made of ice. And that was not what he'd seen in her eyes.

He got up abruptly and turned away. His leg brushed against the table and several of the photos fell to the floor. He left them there.

Crossing to the window, he looked out on the night.

The story was all that mattered. He could not afford to let anything get in the way. Not now, when he was so close to the end of it.

Not when the answers were coming clear.

He felt a rush of exhilaration, knowing that soon

all his efforts would begin to pay off. His persistence, through months of research and investigation, had proven worthwhile. Past dead ends and false leads, he'd pursued the truth of what had happened in this town, and all that remained was the girl.

Paige Seaton Brown had kept her secrets, but in keeping them, she had closed herself off.

He had to convince her to tell him what she knew. . . .

It was cool outside, and he zipped up his jacket as he walked.

The lights were still on in the big house, and he wondered what Charlotte Sinclair was doing up so late. His landlady was an odd one, a dithery, talkative old lady, but she was gone a lot and renting her guest house had certain advantages: she'd given him a key to the main house so he could "check on things" while she was away.

Having the key meant he didn't have to break in to go through her late husband's files.

Frank Sinclair had died a wealthy lawyer, but in 1960 he was the sheriff and he had been the investigating officer in the deaths of Roger and Leigh Chandler Brown.

A year later, the investigation at a standstill, Sinclair resigned.

Six months after that, with money left to him by a distant relative, he enrolled in law school. The inheritance got them through until Sinclair could open his practice.

A very lucky man, Franklin Sinclair.

The ground was spongy beneath his feet, and he made no sound as he walked just beyond the reach of the light which spilled from the windows. He did not see anyone moving inside the house.

The other house was dark.

He stood at the end of the drive and wondered what it had been like, that night.

Soon he would know.

Twenty-three

Stephen was frightened at first, when he heard the lock click, and he began to cry, knowing that he was too old for tears but unable to stop them.

He cried until his eyes stung and he started to cough and gag, bringing up globs of foam and something that looked like snot. That scared him even more, and he threw himself at the door, desperate to get out, and slammed his open hands on the wood.

Gasping, he pulled at the doorknob, but his hands were wet and he could not get a good hold on it. His chest began to ache and he fell to his knees, his face pressed against the door, and tried to think of what to do.

"Breathe, Stevie, take a deep breath," a voice soothed him.

He obeyed, as he'd been taught to do, and gradually he felt better although he had, as always, an uncomfortable feeling that he'd done something very wrong.

The bad voices always told him what he had. . . .

". . . little bastard throws a fit . . ."

". . . I don't think you understand . . ."
". . . hold you responsible . . ."
". . . crazy . . ."
". . . nothing but trouble . . ."

Stephen bit the tip of his tongue until he tasted the warm, salty blood, and the voices faded from his mind.

He lay on his side in front of the door. Sweet, cool air blew into his face and he inhaled eagerly, closing his eyes and imagining that he was back in the woods. He wondered when he would be let out.

He did not want to be locked in again.

MONDAY

Twenty-four

The crime scene drawing had been enlarged and took up most of the bulletin board in the briefing room. It was bordered by several of the more gut-wrenching photographs of the victim.

Noah paced back and forth in front of the display, trying to decide what it was about this murder that didn't seem to fit. It reminded him of one of those puzzles: "What's missing from this picture?"

Only it wasn't the tiger's tail.

He heard the door open behind him and he turned, expecting it to be the desk officer, McClure, with the teletype from the DMV.

Martin Wyatt stood in the doorway.

"Working late again, Noah?"

Noah glanced at his watch and was surprised to see that it was after 1 A.M. "So I am . . . and yourself?"

"The Larson boy has the croup." He came into the room and pulled out a chair. "Scared his parents half to death. It took ten minutes to ease his breathing and half an hour to calm Ruby down."

"Sounds about right."

"So, here I am, wide awake in the middle of the night."

"Here you are," Noah agreed.

Wyatt smiled. "And you're wondering why I'm here."

"It's my nature to be curious."

"And, of course, your job . . ." Wyatt shrugged. "I, too, am curious." He looked past Noah to the photographs, but his face did not register any reaction to what he saw.

"Did you know him?"

"Only in the way that people in small towns sometimes know each other; well enough to say 'hello' to, and talk about the weather."

"Ever been to the tavern?"

"Once or twice, I suppose."

"Weren't you Naomi's doctor?"

"Well, no, actually, I only saw her that one time."

Noah nodded, although he suspected that Naomi might have had a lot to say about her husband on the day she'd been taken, nose bloodied and broken, to see Martin Wyatt. That had been right before she left town.

For a moment neither of them spoke. Wyatt continued to stare at the photographs.

"I haven't seen Ellen lately. How's she doing?"

"She's fine," Wyatt said, "but every once in a while she overdoes it. Our niece was over to supper this afternoon, and it all but wore Ellen out—"

"Your niece . . ." Noah interrupted. "Is she the one?"

"She is."

From the day he'd first arrived in Tranquility, he'd heard talk of "poor little Paige Brown," as though the incident in question had happened yesterday,

rather than having taken place some twenty-odd years before. He was surprised, nonetheless, to find himself interested.

"Well," Wyatt said, getting to his feet, "I guess I'll call it a night." He hesitated, took a step closer to the bulletin board, and then shook his head. "A terrible way to die."

"It is . . . and it kind of makes you wonder . . ."

The look on Martin Wyatt's face was indecipherable. "Wonder?"

"What it was that Bucky Hightower did to make someone mad enough to want to do that to him."

On the way out, Noah stopped by the desk to check on the status of the DMV teletype.

McClure, apparently absorbed in entering data into the department's new computer, did not look up. The teletype itself was silent.

"Did you get a last known address on Naomi Hightower?"

McClure jumped and swung around. "Jesus! You about scared the shit out of me!"

"Sorry. What about Hightower?"

McClure did not get up, but rolled his chair backward across the room to a second desk. He plucked a single sheet of paper from a wire basket, held it a foot in front of his face, and began to read.

"Hightower, Naomi Celeste. Birth date four, twelve, forty-six. Address as of four, twenty, eighty-four is Nineteen-nineteen Hazelwood Drive, in lovely downtown San Jose, California. Female, five feet and oh, a hundred pounds, blond and brown."

McClure winked. "Not bad stats."

"Go on."

"Ah . . . license is valid, no departmental actions, no convictions, no failures to appear . . . no accidents. The lady is a paragon of driving virtue."

Noah smiled. "Sounds like it. Have you been able to turn up a next of kin for Bucky?"

"So far, she's it."

"An ex-wife usually makes a lousy next of kin." Noah took the sheet McClure offered and scanned it.

"You want me to call the San Jose PD and ask them to send an officer to notify her?"

"No . . . I think I'd rather tell her myself."

McClure looked perplexed. "Why? She isn't a suspect, is she?"

"Not a suspect, but maybe a witness." Noah folded the paper and tucked it in his shirt pocket.

McClure blinked. "I don't follow. You think she was here? In town?"

"No."

"Then what could she have seen?"

Noah went around the gate toward the door. "That's what I'm going to ask her."

Twenty-five

Felicity hurried down the stairs in her stockinged feet, and tried not to think about slipping. If she woke her mother up again, she'd never hear the end of it; more importantly, she might be late getting to City Hall. She wanted to do her errands before anyone else arrived. It was only six now.

At the bottom of the stairs she stopped long enough to put on her shoes, then continued out the door. She did not turn to look at the house—what if her mother had managed to get out of her sickbed and was gesturing for her to come back?—nor did she take an easy breath until she was halfway down the block.

"Thank God," she whispered, and rolled her eyes heavenward. "Thank you, too, Jack Daniel's."

A hangover was about the only thing she'd ever known to silence her mother's wrath. . . .

Felicity raised her face to the morning sun and smiled. She felt better, this minute, than she could remember feeling in a very long time.

The keys her mother had given her were labeled

clearly and she had no difficulty getting through the myriad of locks that secured the cluster of offices which comprised the mayor's suite.

Next to the mayor, her mother had the largest, most elaborate office. The sanctum, as mother referred to it, was paneled in dark wood, furnished modernly with a lot of chrome and glass, and had carpet so thick it was hard to walk through.

They had, Felicity noticed, removed the typewriter since the last time she'd visited.

Her mother had won that battle, too.

"I can't type," Lenore O'Hara proclaimed proudly to all who inquired. "Never could type worth a damn."

How had she come to be the mayor's executive secretary? Felicity knew the answer by heart:

"Through attrition. I kept hanging on in there while all the whiz-kid secretaries came and went. I outlasted them, got seniority . . . and the rest is civil service history."

Felicity shivered, hearing the strident tones as clearly as if her mother were standing behind her.

She crossed to the desk and sat down, then unlocked the bottom drawer. Inside the drawer, built in, was a small cabinet with a combination lock. After a quick glance at the numbers her mother had written down for her, she twisted the dial and in a second had it open.

The leather pouch was secured with a lock of its own.

Felicity reached for the pouch, trying to imagine what on earth could be so important, or so valuable, that it needed three locks. Extraordinary precautions,

she thought, for what her mother had referred to as "some paperwork."

Still, it wasn't her concern. She tossed the pouch on the desk and began to lock up.

"Shit!"

Felicity jumped; the voice sounded as if it came from the next room, but she had not heard anyone come in. Even if they had, the rest of the staff was female, and the voice was definitely male. The janitor?

"Will you look at that!" A low whistle followed.

The voice was not coming from the outer office, she realized, but rather from the other direction.

Her mother's office was adjacent to that of the sheriff.

Instinctively, she knew what had prompted the man's astonishment: photographs of poor Mr. Hightower. Try as she might, she hadn't been able to avoid overhearing some of the details of his death. . . .

Sickened, Felicity closed her eyes, but her imagination would not let her be, and her mind filled with horrible visions of blood and gore.

"Come on," a second voice urged, "let's get out of here."

The first man laughed. "What's the matter? Haven't you ever seen a turkey on a spit?"

"Oh, sweet Jesus," she said involuntarily, and then clapped her hand over her mouth.

"Come on . . . if anyone catches us in here . . ."

"All right, all right. I didn't realize that you were such a sensitive guy."

119

"Hey, I'd like to keep this job."

There was a shuffling sound, the jangle of keys, and a moment later she heard a door being closed. Then . . . silence.

When Felicity got to the library, she locked herself in.

Twenty-six

Goldstein entered the store through the back door and walked sedately into the supply room. He took off his suit jacket, arranged it meticulously on a wood hanger, and then selected a freshly laundered apron from the cupboard.

There were customers outside, waiting for him to unlock the doors, but he refused to be hurried. A proper opening required certain preparations, and beginning the business day without them was ill-advised.

For those who were too impatient to allow him his routine, there was always the supermarket with its plastic-wrapped meats and assembly-line produce. And, of course, the delightful ambiance of freeze-dried music.

His store had character.

He opened the wall safe and took out the cash drawer, then carried it out to the register. Although he'd counted the money at closing on Saturday, he licked his thumb and counted it twice again.

Someone jiggled the door handle, and he looked up, annoyed. The shade was drawn and he couldn't see who had done it, but they couldn't see him either, and he made a face.

"In a minute," he said, and pulled out the accounts book to enter a morning total. Then, because the door was again being rattled, he flipped through the pages of a ledger, checking to see which customers had yet to pay their April balances.

At nine-ten, he crossed to the door, unlatched it, and stood back to let his customers in.

Goldstein watched Missy Prentice as she bustled up and down the aisles, her nose in the air.

Instead of using one of the carts, she carried a net shopping bag, which expanded alarmingly as she crammed cans, boxes, and jars into it. It had to be getting heavy, he thought, but apparently not heavy enough to slow her down.

He noticed she hadn't put any perishables into the bag.

"Horace," she said, coming up to the register, "where are your canned meats?"

"Canned meats?"

One eyebrow shot up. "I believe that's what I just asked. You carry them, don't you?"

"Well, I do, but—"

"What aisle?"

He came around the counter and pointed toward the far wall. "Along the back, there, top shelf. Here, I'd better help, I don't think you'll be able to reach

them." He walked along with her and had to dodge the swaying shopping bag.

Once there, they craned their necks to see.

"Give me a couple of those Argentine beef," Missy instructed, and then pointed at an odd-shaped tin with a bright yellow label. "That, too."

Goldstein complied. "I've got the best fresh meat counter in a hundred miles. . . . Why would you want to eat this?" The writing on the yellow label was not in English, but there was a picture of a pig—or it might have been an overweight goat—in the left-hand corner.

"What's that one?"

Irritated, he grabbed a can. "Potted meat," he read, and handed it to her.

She studied it for a moment before shoving it into her bag. "I don't suppose you've got any Spam?"

He repressed a shudder. "I've got a nice rib roast."

"Never mind." She spun on her heel—he had a sudden image of her as a drill sergeant—and marched toward the front of the store. "This'll do."

He studied her as he rang up her purchases, noting that her eyes were puffy and red, and the skin beneath them had darkened and sagged.

Missy had, since he'd known her, looked her age, but this morning she appeared older, worn, almost sickly. Her shoulders were bowed and there was a tremor in her hands as she held her sweater around her. Yet she had toted that shopping bag as if it were filled with goose feathers.

He flipped a can for the price and stared instead at

the label. Canned potatoes? To go with her potted meats?

What was going on?

He cleared his throat and held up the can. "Have they predicted another flood? I mean . . . you're laying in supplies like the end of the world was near."

The look Missy gave him was guarded and her voice, when she spoke, was barely above a whisper. "I may not be able to get out for a while."

"What?"

"I'll be ready for them this time." She looked over her shoulder toward the other customers, none of whom were paying any attention. "I didn't sleep last night, keeping watch."

He shook his head, confused. "Watch on what?"

"Someone's about trouble in this town, Horace. and I'm not going to be a victim."

"You mean that scum, Hightower."

Missy leaned closer to him, and he could feel her breath on his face. "Not only him." She nodded sharply. "Mark my words, there'll be more."

"Oh, I don't—"

"Keep your boy in at night," she interrupted him. "And if you sleep, sleep light."

After Missy left, he had a backup at the register, as the other customers were all ready to check out at the same time, so he didn't have time to think about what she'd said.

But when things quieted down, he began to wonder.

124

Was Missy losing touch? Or was something really happening?

Stephen had been out all night, the night that Hightower was killed.

"Keep your boy in . . ."

Well, he was locked in now.

Twenty-seven

"I thought you were going to San Jose."

Noah looked up. "Joseph . . . I'm just about to leave, as a matter of fact. What can I do for you?" He closed the file folder on Bucky Hightower.

"Ah . . . I wanted to talk to you, about yesterday."

"All right. Have a seat." He had an idea what was coming, but hoped he was wrong. Joe had only been on the force for six months. . . .

Ramos sat on the edge of the chair. "I'll get straight to the point. I don't think I'm cut out for this job."

Damn, he thought, but only said, "How so?"

"You saw me." Ramos's voice sounded ragged. "I only just kept from tossin' my cookies."

"It was pretty rough," Noah acknowledged.

"Rough." The deputy seemed to consider the word. "For you it was rough, for me it was a nightmare. I've seen people maimed and killed in car accidents, but this . . ." He swallowed and looked away.

Noah waited it out.

"It was slaughter," Ramos continued a moment later. "The law can call it homicide, the papers'll call

it murder, but that was a God-damned slaughter. I know, intellectually, that things like that happen, but I don't want my face rubbed in it. I think I'd better get out."

"You've made up your mind?"

"I have."

Noah frowned. "I'm sorry to lose you. I think you've got the makings of a good cop."

Ramos laughed unsteadily. "A fair-weather cop, suitable for issuing traffic tickets and arresting drunks."

"If you want to stay with the department, I can transfer you to the desk."

"No, I . . . my wife and I talked about it last night . . . I couldn't sleep . . . and we've, *I've* decided to try San Francisco. Her dad's got an insurance office and she's been after me to go to work for him." He shrugged. "Nine to five, Monday through Friday, three-piece suits . . . and the worst injury I can imagine dealing with there would be a paper cut."

Noah thought it sounded like hell. "I understand, Joe, and I wish you luck." He stood up and extended his hand.

Ramos looked flustered. "I'm really sorry."

Noah watched him leave.

The day was getting off to a lousy start.

He adjusted the shoulder holster and was reaching for his jacket when he heard the door behind him open.

"Excuse me . . . Sheriff Clayton?"

He turned to see an attractive dark-haired woman

standing in the doorway. She was dressed in white linen slacks and a dark blue silk blouse.

"Yes?"

"I'm Paige Brown."

Noah knew she was a doctor, but thought it to her credit that she didn't introduce herself that way. "Noah Clayton. Is there something I can help you with?"

"I have something I'd like to show you." She held out a thick manila envelope. Her expression indicated that the "something" was not good.

He accepted the envelope and took it to his desk to open. The contents were a surprise. They were unmistakably crime scene photographs. Some were quite graphic.

"Where did you get these?"

"They were pushed under my front door."

He glanced at her and realized that she was exerting a great deal of self-control, but there was anger in her gray eyes. "Do you know who did it?"

"A writer who approached me for an interview—"

"Austin?"

"You know him?"

Noah shook his head. "I know *of* him. So this is what he was after." He gathered the photographs in a pile and started to put them back into the envelope.

"What I want to know is where he got them."

"Hmm?"

"These are obviously police photographs."

"Yes, I'd say so."

"Where did he get them? I mean, the sheriff's department doesn't routinely release this type of material."

"No, we certainly don't but—"

"Then how does someone . . . how did *he* . . . get those pictures? Aren't they confidential?"

Belatedly, he understood. "I see what you're getting at," he said thoughtfully. "Maybe I'd better have a talk with Mr. Austin."

She lifted her chin. "Talk with him?"

"Talk with him," he confirmed.

It appeared to him that her eyes darkened, turning a stormier shade of gray. What was she mad about? Had she expected him to run out and arrest Cody Austin?

"I wonder, Sheriff Clayton, if he got the photographs from your office."

Noah laughed in spite of himself. "No, he did not."

"You're sure of that?"

"I am." He handed her the envelope. "Look, I can see that you're upset about this, and I don't blame you at all, but Austin didn't, as far as I can see, break the law."

"That you know of."

He shrugged. "I will talk to him when I get a chance . . ." He saw her eyes flash and felt a surge of annoyance. "I've got a fresh murder on my hands, a murderer to find, and one of my deputies just quit. I'm afraid I can't get too excited about an overambitious writer who's stumbled onto some photographs of a long-forgotten crime . . ."

"I haven't forgotten it."

He stopped short. "I'm sorry."

She lowered her eyes for a moment, and when she looked up he saw something wild and hurting there,

130

and he felt an aching response of his own.

God, he thought.

"Thank you for your time," she said.

It was nearly ten-thirty before he managed to get free of the office.

He brought along Bucky's rapidly expanding case file and a copy of the report pertaining to the High-tower's "domestic dispute" in 1984.

Among the statements quoted in the 1984 report was a threat by Naomi against her husband's life: "It may take a while, you bastard, but I'm going to get you for this."

According to the officer who'd been at the scene, Bucky's reply had been, "Try it, bitch."

Had she tried?

Twenty-eight

For the first time since he'd started his practice in 1962, Martin canceled his morning appointments at the office and then disappeared into the den, closing the door behind him.

Ellen hadn't the faintest idea what was going on, but she instinctively didn't like it. She wandered aimlessly through the house—her own schedule had been disrupted—and cast occasional questioning glances at the ceiling.

What was he up to?

Why had he chosen today, of all days, to stay home?

She stopped in the living room, plumped the cushions on the sofa, and then ever-so-carefully lifted the phone from the cradle and brought it to her ear. A dial tone. She hung up.

Frowning, Ellen tried to recall if he had said anything yesterday about staying home today, but yesterday was mostly a blur in her mind . . . except that she remembered Paige had been over for Sunday dinner.

Had it something to do with her niece? But what could that be?

Bits of conversation came back to her, none of it clear, and now she regretted the wine-induced oblivion that she'd purposely sought.

She shook her head in irritation. Useless, trying to recapture a moment in time, particularly when what really mattered was what to do *now*.

She had taken the last of the Valium, and she needed Martin out of the house so that she could get one of his prescription pads. This time she would increase the medication strength from five to ten milligrams, and order a hundred pills instead of forty.

Her pulse quickened as she thought of it; when she'd last gotten a refill, the pharmacist had commented that she'd gone through forty pills in an awful hurry. She had stammered and finally said that she'd dropped some of them down the sink.

She would have to go to a different pharmacy.

If anyone questioned the prescription—the quantity might be considered unusual—she would say that she was going abroad for several months and needed enough medication to last her.

"Did you hear me, Ellen? I'm leaving now."

Ellen started; she had been so absorbed in her plans that she hadn't heard him come downstairs.

"Are you all right?"

"Yes," she said, and forced a smile. "I was just . . . lost in thought."

Martin nodded but she had the distinct impression that he was preoccupied and had not really heard her reply.

134

"I may be late tonight." He moved toward the door. "Try to get some rest today."

Even that directive seemed automatic, performed by rote, and she watched after him, curious as to what thoughts *he* was lost in.

Martin had locked the den.

She was annoyed, but it was a minor annoyance; she'd had the locksmith out to make a key for the dead bolt the day after her husband had installed it.

Ellen hurried to the bedroom and dug through her jewelry box for the key. The sharp point of a brooch stabbed beneath her right thumbnail and she sucked at the blood which welled up as she walked back down the hall.

The key turned smoothly in the lock.

Once inside, she looked around the room, wondering what Martin had wanted to hide. There was nothing noticeably out of place, no mysterious crates or packages, no smoking gun. . . .

No, she thought, that was not fair of her. Martin was a good man who once had been forced by circumstances to act against his conscience.

What he'd done, he'd done for both of them.

She mustn't forget that.

Ellen found a prescription pad in the top drawer of the desk and tore off a blank.

Her thumb throbbed painfully as she wrote out the order, but the bleeding had stopped and, if anything, the shakiness of her hand made her writing look more

like his than usual. Forging the signature was easy; after so many years of marriage, she could sign his name better than he could.

Folding the slip of paper, she tucked it in her skirt pocket.

Soon now, she promised herself, soon.

Twenty-nine

San Jose was as dismal as he remembered it.

What was it about California, he wondered, that made its cities sprawl? Once upon a time, not that many years ago, it had been possible to detect visually where one town ended and another began. Now the lines of demarcation were indistinct, and it was not uncommon to live in a different city than the neighbor across the street.

Naomi Hightower lived in a wood-frame house on a quiet street near the city limits. How long the street would remain quiet was debatable; condos, in the last stages of construction, loomed menacingly in the background.

Noah parked and got out of the car, then glanced upward at the hazy sky. The sun was almost directly overhead.

As he approached the house, he noticed a curtain being pulled aside, but whoever was looking out at him stood far enough back to be out of view.

A second later, as he went up the steps, the door swung open.

Through the screen he could see her. Dressed in

blue jeans and a bright red halter top, with her blond hair worn long and straight, the former Mrs. Bucky Hightower looked more like a teenager than a forty-year-old woman.

"Naomi."

"Sheriff." She lit a cigarette and then nudged the screen door open with a bare foot. "Come in."

He stepped inside and she immediately turned away, walking ahead of him into the front room.

"I thought you might be coming by," she said, and flopped onto the couch.

"Oh?" He sat opposite her. In this light he could see more clearly that the face didn't match the body. Too many years spent worshiping the sun?

As if aware of his scrutiny, she leaned back, into the shadows, and blew a cloud of smoke between them. "Tell me . . . did the bastard suffer?"

"So you know Bucky's dead."

Naomi nodded. "You'll pardon me if I don't cry."

"How did you find out?"

Her smile flashed, white and vicious. "Lenore called me."

"When was this?"

"Oh . . . early afternoon, yesterday." She shrugged. "I didn't make a note of the time."

"And that was the first you'd heard of it?"

"Yes." She leaned forward and tapped a long ash into an opened can of beer, one of many on the glass coffee table, and it occurred to him that she kept house much the way her ex-husband had.

Noah took out a note pad and flipped it to a blank page. "When was the last time you saw Bucky?"

She narrowed her eyes, then tapped the side of her

nose with a red-nailed index finger. "When he gave me this," she said, indicating a small but noticeable bump. "Broke it."

"You left that day?" That was something of a surprise; for some reason he'd thought otherwise.

"I did. I *should* have left long before that, but I kept thinking . . ." She smiled and pushed back her hair. "Anyway, when he broke my nose, I knew it was time to get out." She touched the bump gingerly. "This was my birthday present."

Noah remembered the dates from the DMV report; she'd changed her address a little more than a week after turning thirty-eight.

She laughed. "Happy birthday to me, right?" She took a last puff of her cigarette—an unfiltered Camel—and dropped it into a can, then matched the hiss with one of her own. "God, I hope he suffered."

"It wasn't pleasant."

"Hmm." Her eyes glittered as she extracted a cigarette from a fresh pack. "Lousy bastard."

"After you left, did you have any contact with him?"

"No."

Studying her, he wondered. "You didn't see him in court? For the divorce?"

"He defaulted." She picked a shred of tobacco off her lip and flicked it away. "Good thing he did. My lawyer had it on him, coming and going."

"Had what on him?"

She didn't answer right away, instead watching the smoke curl from her cigarette.

Noah tried again. "What did you have on him?"

Her face became pouty, a look that he found

unattractive from a woman her age. "This is a murder case," he said, "and I intend to investigate very thoroughly. I wouldn't advise you to hold anything back."

"Shit."

He waited.

"Well, actually, it was mostly bluff on my part . . ."

"What was?"

"I let him think I knew what his secrets were." She sighed. "Bucky liked to drink, and once in a while he'd wallow in the booze, get a little amorous, and then he'd start to talk. You know . . ."

Sensing it was required of him, Noah nodded.

"He'd ramble on about something or the other until he passed out. The next day he wouldn't remember what he'd said, and he always asked me, kind of nervous."

"Go on."

"I thought at first there was another woman, and what he was nervous about . . . was letting something slip." She laughed and swept back her hair with a caressing gesture that looked practiced to him. "I shouldn't have worried . . . no other woman would have him."

That didn't say much for her, Noah thought, but didn't comment.

"Anyway, I'd tell him what he said, and then he'd try to pass it off like he had nothing to hide. But it happened enough times to convince him that he *did* run off at the mouth when he got plastered. And to convince me that he *was* hiding something."

"So what did he tell you?"

"Actually . . . nothing. But"—she smiled modestly—"I pretended he had. I just would give him this dead-serious look and say, *I know, Bucky*, and he'd back off. My drama teacher always told me I should've been an actress."

It wasn't what Noah wanted to hear.

She got up off the couch and leaned over to gather several of the empty beer cans in her hands, taking her time at it as if to allow him the opportunity to admire her cleavage. "Hey, you want a beer?"

"No thanks."

"Mind if I—"

"Go ahead."

This time her smile could only be called provocative, and when she walked out of the room, it was with a definite sway.

"You know," she called from the kitchen, "I used to see you driving around, and I always wondered what a guy like you was doing in that two-bit town."

Noah frowned at that and decided to ignore it. "So you never found out what he was hiding?"

Naomi came back into the room, popping the top of her beer. "No, but it must've been something big, illegal maybe. Even my lawyer said so. It would have to be to keep him from contesting the divorce settlement and all."

"Do you have any idea of who might have killed him? Who might have had a reason to want him dead?"

"No one wanted that more than I did, but I didn't kill him." She tucked her legs under her and leaned

141

forward again. "If I had, you'd still be running around picking up the pieces . . ."

He left a short time later, more or less convinced that Naomi Hightower had not been involved in her ex-husband's death. Oddly, it was her intense hostility toward Bucky that brought him to that conclusion; he believed her when she said that if Hightower had died by her hand, it would have been a much worse death.

Naomi hadn't been scorned, but Hell's fury indeed paled in comparison to her own.

He also believed her statement that she didn't know any of Bucky's secrets. If she had, she would've taken pleasure revealing them.

All of which left him precisely where he had started . . . without a suspect.

Thirty

At first Paige had tried to keep her feelings in check by channeling them into what Alex referred to as her "doctor anger"—which was cold, clipped, and definitely controlled—but when that didn't work, she allowed herself to get mad.

The more she thought about it, the madder she became.

By the time she got home she was furious, both at Austin and the sheriff, and she vented that anger by slamming a few doors.

She could hear Alex now: *"Rather childish, don't you think?"*

No, she didn't think . . .

"Safe, then, without confrontation?"

But she hadn't come home to stir things up . . .

"Then why . . . what did you hope to accomplish by running home?"

She wasn't running . . .

"Aren't you? Aren't you? Aren't . . ."

"Leave me alone, Alex," she said out loud.

The voice which answered was her own: *"You don't want to be alone."*

143

And it was true.

Paige stopped slamming doors.

She'd never told Alex, or anyone else, but for a while she had gone to a psychiatrist, trying to work through her problems. For sixteen months, an hour at a time, twice a week, she'd focused inward, looking for answers to questions never asked.

The psychiatrist, a Dr. Reynoso, sat behind his desk, head propped up in his hand, and listened, generally without comment, as she talked about her life. Occasionally one of his eyebrows would arch and he would nod and say, "I see."

She admitted to him that part of the reason she'd become a doctor was so that she'd never need to depend on anyone to take care of her, because she'd learned that sometimes they weren't there when you needed them.

She told him that, at age nine and about a year after her parents' deaths, she'd found herself angry with them for leaving her. She hadn't told anyone and she managed to hide her feelings largely by denying to herself and others that she felt anything at all.

By the time she was thirteen, she told him, she had become very adept at imposing distance between herself and anyone trying to get close to her. Not even her grandmother, whom she'd loved dearly, was allowed "in."

Dr. Reynoso steepled his hands and looked over the tips of his fingers at her, and then said, "I understand."

Which made her think she was making progress.

Preparing for college and later medical school

144

provided her with the perfect excuse for her semi-reclusive behavior. No one questioned her; it was assumed that she was simply a dedicated young woman who was too busy for the distractions that a social life might bring.

No one ever asked her if she was lonely.

When, at age twenty-eight, after fifteen years of study and sacrifice, she achieved her goal and had become a doctor, she found less satisfaction than she'd expected.

Her choice of specialty—emergency medicine—allowed her to help people without really becoming involved with them. She never called her patients by their first names, because they were strangers to her, and she to them.

Even the nurses she worked with were strangers. Because she was the doctor . . . the hardworking doctor who had no time for a drink after a rough night.

After her second year on staff, her isolation was nearly complete.

Alex had tried to break that isolation, determinedly seeking her out. When he saw her at a hospital function, he made a point of talking with her.

"You look like you could use a friend," he explained, and became one.

He was there for her when she broke down one day after a three-year-old girl had been brought in DOA, the victim of a brutal beating and sexual assault. He held her as she cried for the girl and all the lost children, even herself. He took her home and listened to the anger and guilt that poured out of her wounded heart.

Then for a short while they were lovers, a new

experience for her and seemingly an obsession for him. She was afraid to break it off, because she truly cared for him and didn't want to hurt their friendship, but their lovemaking left her empty and wanting. . . .

She stopped sleeping with Alex at about the same time she stopped seeing the psychiatrist.

Paige went upstairs to her old room, and stood in the doorway trying to remember what it felt like to be whole. In a matter of minutes everything she loved had been taken from her. Her sense of loss was acute, as if it had been days and not years since that morning.

Why had she come home? To search for the part of her that had died that day?

"One of these days you'll have to stop running and just deal with it," Alex had told her. "I don't think you've ever really faced what happened."

Was he right?

About the first, yes; she'd been running all of her life.

And the other? Did she even *know* what really happened? She'd been so young then, sheltered. No one talked about it to her, and they stopped talking among themselves if she came into the room.

Did anyone know? The murders were unsolved.

Cody Austin had implied that he knew the truth about her parents' deaths.

Perhaps it was time that she did too.

Thirty-one

"How is your mother feeling?"

Felicity looked up to see Charlotte Sinclair smiling sweetly, plump arms full of overdue books. Charlotte was well known as a notoriously slow reader and her fines had paid for many of the library's new acquisitions.

"She's fine, Mrs. Sinclair," Felicity said quietly, "thank you for asking."

"She has the flu that's going around?" The older woman dumped the books on the counter and started digging in her purse, presumably for her wallet.

"I guess so." When Felicity had gone home at lunchtime, she'd found her mother feeling worse.

"Well, tell Lenore I asked after her, and I hope she's better soon."

Felicity nodded, adding up the late charges. "That'll be eleven dollars . . . ten books at five cents a day for twenty-two days."

Charlotte shook her head. "One of these days I'll remember to bring my books back before I leave on vacation," she said, and held out a twenty.

Felicity knew better than to start Mrs. Sinclair

talking about her vacations. She made change and handed it over without comment, then glanced at her watch. Five o'clock . . . quitting time.

The woman started off toward the reference desk but stopped a few feet away.

Felicity looked after her, dreading the possibility that she might come back, and then saw him. . . .

"Oh, Mr. Austin," Charlotte said, "a small world, isn't it?"

Felicity kept herself busy until he went out the door, then followed as unobtrusively as she could.

He was standing at the foot of the stairs and she hesitated at the top, feeling her heartbeat quicken at the thought that he might turn and see her.

A patrol car pulled to a stop at the curb beside him.

Felicity turned, took a step backward, and opened her purse, hoping that it looked as if she were searching for her keys. . . .

Out of the corner of her eye, she saw Noah Clayton get out of the car.

"You're Cody Austin," Noah said, but Felicity thought that it didn't sound like a question.

"Yes."

"Would you mind coming over to my office? I'd like to talk to you."

"Is there a problem?"

She couldn't keep herself from staring at him. Cody Austin. Even his name was . . .

The sheriff looked in her direction, and she spun on her heel, moving quickly toward the library door.

". . . a problem, but I have a few questions . . ."

The door cut off the rest of the conversation.

Her mouth suddenly dry, Felicity remembered how clearly she'd heard the voices from the sheriff's office, and she knew that she would go there.

The prospect of learning more about Cody Austin was irresistible.

Thirty-two

"Have a seat," Noah said, and crossed to the desk, where he glanced through a small stack of messages. Nothing urgent and nothing from the lab.

"I have to say, Sheriff, I'm surprised you know my name."

Noah looked at Austin, who sat opposite him, seemingly at ease. "I make it my business to know who's in my town."

Austin's amusement was evident. "That sounds like a line from a B-grade movie."

"Attending to business, I did a little checking." Noah consulted the folder he'd requested from records after Paige Brown had left his office. "Austin, Cody, no middle name. Journalism major in college, worked as a stringer for Associated Press and as an investigative reporter for various newspapers in Southern California. Also did legwork for a PI firm. As far as we can determine, right now you're not working for anyone . . ."

"That's right." The amused look had disappeared.

"You showed up here last November, just the weekends at first, most of which you spent either in

the library or wandering around. You've since rented the guest house at the Sinclair place."

"Do you make it a practice to conduct surveillance on everyone who comes here?"

Noah shook his head. "Not surveillance, per se, but"—he smiled—"it's a small town and people notice things."

"Obviously." There was resentment in the word. Strange, Noah thought, considering that Austin had made a career out of noticing things himself.

"Mr. Austin, let me just come right out and ask you . . . what are you doing in Tranquility?"

"I'm researching a book."

"Really? On what?"

"The 1960 murders . . . Roger and Leigh Brown."

"Has someone commissioned your book?"

"If you mean, do I have a contract with a publisher for it, the answer is no."

"Then you're working on your own."

"I prefer to work that way."

"You've written other books, then."

Austin started at him for a moment before answering. "No, I haven't. I don't see what that has to do with anything."

"Maybe nothing." Noah leaned back in the chair. "So what is all this about?"

"Attending to business. Mr. Austin, how did you come to be in possession of official police photographs of the Brown crime scene?"

"Oh." Austin looked relieved. "That."

Noah waited.

"Well, it was simple, really. I tracked down the photographer, or rather his wife; he died in 1972. She

152

had a trunk full of his stuff. . . . I found the negatives and had new prints made."

"I see."

"You can check it out if you want to. There was nothing illegal about it."

"Mr. Austin, do you think," Noah said carefully, "that it was ethical or moral to give copies of those photographs to Paige Brown?"

Austin glanced away quickly, and then back. "I thought she had a right to know."

"The press is big on the 'right to know.' To the point of shoving it down our throats sometimes."

"I think you're taking a very narrow view," Austin said.

"Maybe. But you haven't answered my question."

"I violated no standard of ethics . . ."

"And you think what you did is morally defensible?"

"I wasn't aware that morality was part of your jurisdiction, Sheriff. Law enforcement needs to clean up its own act before criticizing the press."

"I wouldn't pass around pictures of a murder scene without considering the consequences, emotional or otherwise."

Austin got up from the chair and thrust his hands in his pockets. "This is amazing; I'm being lectured on sensitivity by a cop. I've read about how *sensitive* you guys are when you take relatives to the morgue to identify a body. I think that's far worse—"

"Don't believe everything you read or see in the movies, Mr. Austin."

"I'm capable of reaching my own conclusions."

"Journalists usually are," Noah observed dryly.

"But what I'm saying is, Dr. Brown was disturbed by those pictures—anyone would be—and I think you crossed the line between your right to know, as you call it, and her right not to be harassed."

"Have I broken the law?"

Noah didn't like the man's tone of voice, but he could hardly arrest him for that. "No, not the law, but like I said, this is a small town . . . you may find it uncomfortable if word about what you've done gets out."

Austin held his hands up in surrender. "You've made your point. . . . I won't do it again."

"No, I know you won't." Noah closed the folder and pushed it out of his way. "But just in case . . . I'll be watching."

After Austin left, Noah started to write the report on his interview with Naomi Hightower, but found it hard to concentrate. His mind kept wandering and he realized after a moment that Austin had gotten to him.

Austin had, unknowingly, touched a nerve. What had he really said, though? Something about having read about an insensitive cop. No big deal, but the perception of police officers as some kind of emotion-less mutants had long been a sore spot.

Seventeen years in law enforcement and Noah hadn't yet formed a scab.

Part of it was the frequent portrayal of cops as booze-brained loners with a penchant for shooting unarmed juveniles. How many times had he read books where the cop hero was trying to forget a

shoot-out in a darkened alley?

Oh, he knew there were cases like that, but if it happened as often as some novelist needed a reason for a character to brood, being blown away by a trigger-happy cop would be the leading cause of death for adolescents.

Maybe policemen should follow the lead of other minorities, and protest the unfavorable depiction of cops in film and fiction. Of course, the way things were going, before long there would be nobody left to be the bad guys in the movies.

He was more tired than he realized; his thoughts were getting away from him.

"Time to call it a night," he said aloud.

Noah locked up the office and started down the hall. As he turned the corner he nearly collided with a woman hurrying in the opposite direction.

"Excuse me." He offered a steadying hand.

"Oh!" She glanced at him, then lowered her eyes, her face coloring almost instantly. "My fault," she stammered, and then ducked around him and was gone.

He wondered idly what Felicity was doing in the building so late—the city offices had been closed for over an hour—and then dismissed it from his mind.

"Keep it quiet tonight," he said to the desk officer as he headed for the door.

"Absolutely," McClure responded. "Dead quiet."

Thirty-three

The noise the crushed rock made as he walked over it reminded Goldstein of the sound his spine would make when he finally had a chance to unkink it.

It had been an unusually long day—his afternoon clerk had called in sick—and his back had cramped up in the middle of ringing up Charlotte Sinclair's order. He had never seen anything like it; she'd bought enough food to feed the Russian army.

Small wonder the woman looked like a pork sausage ready to bust its casing.

Goldstein dug into his pocket for the house keys. Looking at the darkened house, he felt a twinge of guilt. He hadn't been able to get home to let the boy out for lunch, but then *he* hadn't had time to eat either.

Never mind, he thought, the boy was sturdy enough to do without for a while. And being hungry all day might have been just the thing to reinforce the notion, in Stephen's mind, that he was being punished.

Reinforce. Another psychiatric buzz word he'd heard too many times over the last five and a half years.

Inside the house the air was warm and stuffy, and he left the front door open to cool things off, then stripped off his jacket. His shirt clung to him damply, and he started to unbutton it as he headed down the hall to the back bedroom.

As he neared the door he listened, but there was no sound coming from the room.

He unlocked the dead bolt and twisted the doorknob. The door swung open.

The room was dark and he narrowed his eyes, not in the least bit inclined to go in. If he'd had any such intentions, he would have been dissuaded by the *smell* that wafted out.

It smelled worse than the nut hospital, he thought. There was something feral about the odor, as if he'd come upon the lair of a night animal.

"Stephen?"

A soft rustling came from the far left corner and he could make out the pale circle of his son's face.

Goldstein took a step back and waved a hand in front of him in an attempt to dispel the stench.

"Go clean up," he ordered, "and then come to eat."

Then, without another look, he turned and strode down the hall.

Goldstein stood in front of the stove, meat fork in hand, and peered through the glass at their dinner, two thick sirloin steaks. He'd decided on steak more

because it was easy to fix than from a sense of guilt, but now that it was cooking, he found a strange satisfaction in his choice.

Not that Stephen would know the difference; the boy ate what was put in front of him, apparently unaware of quality. A burned chop was eaten with the same disgusting appetite as filet mignon.

Goldstein sighed and scratched at his neck, fingering a small welt which he assumed was an insect bite. The house had cooled off, but leaving the door open at this time of year was an invitation to the bugs that bred down by the creek.

Thinking of the creek reminded him of the boy; water had been running in the bathroom for a good fifteen minutes. Since the water heater was only good for about ten minutes of hot water, Stephen was showering cold.

Well, as long as he gets clean, Goldstein thought.

The water was still running five minutes later when Goldstein pulled the steaks from the broiler. He forked them onto plates and then ran water—cold water—into the pan.

What was the idiot doing in there?

Probably forgot where he was. Probably waiting for the "rain" to stop.

Well, he didn't intend to eat a cold steak.

But two bites later, the sound of running water was suddenly more than he could take, and he lurched to his feet, knocking the chair over, and thundered down the hall.

The bathroom door stood open.

The shower curtain gaped.

Water beat against the tiles.

Stephen was nowhere in sight, but puddles led out of the room toward the front door. . . .

Dumbfounded, Goldstein could only stare.

Thirty-four

Felicity slowed as she neared the house, looking at the strange car which was parked in the drive. In the fading light of dusk she was unable to tell the color, but it was a big car, most likely American and, she thought, new.

Which of her mother's *friends* had a car like that? Foolish question. It had to be the mayor, the Honorable Charles Light, although she thought she'd heard that he was out of town on some junket.

Were they starting up again?

How many times while she was growing up had she come home to find him making himself comfortable in their front room? How many knowing, leering smiles had she endured?

God, she hated him, and all the others.

One of her earliest memories was of praying for a father so she would be like the rest of the kids. She used to daydream that her father, her real father, would come back one day, but then someone (not her mother) told her that her father would never come back, that he was dead, was dead before she was even born, and she'd stopped daydreaming and stopped

praying, and tried not to think about him at all.

Making a face, she walked quickly by the car—the motor was still pinging, so it couldn't have been here long—and up the steps.

She could hear voices . . . male and female. Were they in the front room?

Taking a deep breath, she opened the door. Her mother, paler than she'd been at lunch, was reclining on the sofa. The man's back was to her, but when he turned, Felicity sighed in relief.

"Dr. Wyatt," she said, "I'm so—"

"Leave us alone," her mother interrupted, and started to get up from where she lay.

"It's all right, Lenore," Dr. Wyatt said. "I'm sure Felicity is concerned about your health." His smile wavered. To her, he said, "Perhaps you should leave, though. You don't want to catch what your mother has."

He had no idea how true that was.

Felicity looked from the doctor to her mother. "I'll just, just—"

"Go!" Lenore rasped, and then began to cough.

She fled, and a moment later, standing motionless in the hallway, she opened and then slammed her bedroom door.

Let them think she was in her room.

"You're sick, Lenore, and you'd be well advised to stay in bed." The doctor's voice carried clearly to where she hid in the kitchen.

"That's why I called you." There was impatience in her mother's response. "Give me something so I

can get back to the office. A shot, or an antibiotic . . ."

"You've got a viral infection; antibiotics won't help."

"Then what will?"

"About a week in bed."

"I haven't time for that. There are things I need to take care of."

There was a long silence before Dr. Wyatt spoke again. "I thought all of that had been . . . done."

"Well, it's come undone."

"How can that be?"

Her mother's laugh sounded as if it hurt. "It can be and it is. Our friend saw to that."

"But . . . how?"

"You know how."

"The papers were destroyed, I saw him do it."

"He *said* he'd destroyed all of them, but—" She coughed, gasped, and in a weaker voice continued, "—do you want to take that chance?"

"No, no. I can't . . ."

"Neither can any of us. But there's no telling what the damned fool might've hung on to, thinking he'd up the ante or just out of stupidity. Lord knows he was dumb enough to do about anything."

"Then let me take care of it. . . . You're in no condition to do anything. I'll do whatever needs to be done. But damn it, Lenore, this has got to be the end of it."

Her mother did not respond and Felicity moved closer, listening intently, but heard nothing more.

From her room she watched as the doctor backed

his car out of the driveway and then drove off down the street. She watched the taillights disappear.

More than a little confused, Felicity turned away from the window and stared absently at her reflection in the mirror across the room.

It was curious, she thought, that in all of her life there had been an absence of mystery, and now, out of the blue, she found herself on the periphery of two of them.

The first, involving her mother, Dr. Wyatt, and unnamed others, revolved around a "friend" and his "papers." Who was the friend, she wondered. What papers? Did the locked leather pouch she'd picked up at her mother's office have anything to do with it? But no, her mother had opened the pouch and all Felicity had seen were accounting sheets and ledgers.

At the center of the other mystery was Cody Austin and an unsolved murder. . . .

Thirty-five

Noah reached into the patrol car and turned off the flashing lights, not wanting to scare the boy if he was hiding somewhere nearby.

The heat of day had given way and there was a definite chill in the air. He tried to imagine what would make a sixteen-year-old walk—dripping wet from a shower—out into the night.

Horace Goldstein, if he knew his son's reasons, was not talking. The grocer stood on the porch, arms folded across his chest, answering in monosyllables to questions put to him by the deputy.

Noah walked toward them, their voices momentarily drowned out by the sound of a third car pulling into the drive.

It was Martin Wyatt. In the faint light it was hard to make out his expression, but there was something about the way the doctor moved that suggested annoyance.

Noah frowned and looked from Wyatt to Goldstein, who made a slight gesture—which might have meant anything or nothing—before turning away.

"Sheriff . . ." Up close, Wyatt's face held the

aloofness of a casual passerby.

"What brings you out this way?"

"Oh . . ." The doctor dug in a pocket and brought out a small vial, holding it up for inspection. "Just bringing by Mr. Goldstein's nitroglycerin." Wyatt raised his voice. "Horace, I brought your medication over since you didn't get by the office to pick it up."

Goldstein hesitated only a second. "Thanks," he said, "I guess it slipped my mind."

Noah had the distinct impression that the exchange between the two men had been for his benefit. It made him curious.

"What's going on?" Wyatt asked.

"Stephen's gone off, just disappeared." Goldstein answered before Noah could reply.

Noah saw a flicker of relief in the doctor's eyes and wondered what answer Wyatt had expected. Something worse, obviously, than a runaway boy.

Still, when Wyatt spoke, the concern in his voice sounded real. "Is there anything I can do to help?"

"Thank you, Dr. Wyatt," Noah said, "but I think we can handle it."

Wyatt nodded and handed the vial to Goldstein. "Well, then, I'll be going, but call if—"

"I will," Goldstein said quickly.

"Show me the boy's room."

Goldstein, who in Noah's opinion had remained remarkably calm throughout the report-taking process, looked startled.

"What?"

"I'd like to see your son's bedroom."

166

Goldstein drew a hand through his wavy hair. "He was in the shower . . . I don't see . . . his footprints were straight from the bathroom to the front door . . ."

Noah shook his head. "It's possible that he finished with his shower, left the water running, went back to his room, and got dressed."

"But his footprints were wet," Goldstein protested.

"He might have gone back to the bathroom and got his feet wet to throw you off-track."

"But . . . he's not that smart." Goldstein averted his eyes. "I told you, he has problems."

"Just the same."

The grocer opened his mouth and then closed it. "All right."

The room that Goldstein showed him to was like something out of a nightmare.

It stank of urine and unwashed bodies.

The windows had been covered with a charcoal-colored reflective film which would, Noah guessed, effectively cut the amount of light coming from outside, and keep the room dark even during the day.

A narrow bed—the only furniture—was against a wall and was heaped with sheets and blankets, none of which looked too clean. Clothes were scattered across the floor. The closet door was secured with a padlock.

Goldstein had remained in the hall.

Noah turned to face him, but it was a moment before he'd controlled his anger enough to speak. "This is how your son lives?"

Goldstein's jaw tightened. "It was clean when I brought him home from the hospital. I'm not responsible for what he's done in here."

"How about the lock on the door? Do you lock him in? Is that why the room smells of piss? Because you lock him in and he can't get out?"

"What the hell do you know?" The man's eyes bulged and his face turned a dusky shade of red. "He got kicked out of that nut house because the doctors said he wasn't crazy enough and they needed his bed. So they sent him home and he'd forgotten how to feed himself. Wash himself. They had him in diapers, for God's sake!"

"You think your son is crazy?"

"How should I know? I think the *doctors* are crazy, I can tell you that. Kicking him out while I'm paying good money, *good money*, for private care. But no. After I pay out a fortune they come to me and say, 'Take him home, Mr. Goldstein, he's not crazy enough.'"

Noah regarded him, trying to assimilate this new information. For some reason, he'd thought that the boy had been away at a private school. "I'd like the names and phone numbers of your son's doctors—"

"All you'll get from them is double-talk!" Spittle had gathered at the corners of his mouth, and Goldstein wiped a hand across his lips. "But they're the ones to blame for this. They took a ten-year-old kid and turned him into an animal."

Noah went to the office and, after repeated tries, managed to get through to the ranking doctor at the

168

private mental hospital where Stephen had been a patient.

"I don't know how much I can help you," a sleepy voice said, "and still protect the patient's rights to confidentiality—he is a minor, after all—but I'll try."

"What was his diagnosis?"

"Well, that's one of the things that I can't say. Hospital policy, I'm afraid."

"Even under these circumstances? With consent from the father?"

"Even so. You can get a court order, perhaps, but it's much more difficult with juveniles. . . . Often the parents fail to comprehend the damage that can be done by releasing sensitive information of this nature. The court would have to be convinced that the circumstances warranted disclosure."

"Can you tell me why he was discharged?"

"Economics. He was in a private room and the hospital decided it could do better by putting a second bed in the room . . ."

"But couldn't he have stayed?"

The doctor chuckled. "Our bed situation is extremely tight. We've got a waiting list to get in here. Stevie was the last of our patients to have a single room. And the next several patients on the waiting list were female. We couldn't have that. . . . We did offer Mr. Goldstein the option of paying for a dual occupancy, so to speak, but he couldn't afford it, so we discharged Stevie."

"What was his condition on release?"

"It was determined," the doctor said carefully, "that he was not a danger to himself or others, and

that he could be treated on an out-patient basis."

"Has he been seen as an out-patient?"

"Not by us. And"—there was the sound of pages being turned—"we haven't sent his records to anyone. That would indicate, to me, that he's not under anyone's care."

"Considering that he may not be undergoing treatment . . . in your opinion . . . would you stand by that determination? That he's not a danger to himself?"

The doctor's voice was guarded. "Well, I couldn't be certain, but—this is only my opinion, mind you—I would say . . . no. I don't think Stevie is dangerous."

TUESDAY

Thirty-six

Missy cupped cold water in her hands and brought it up to her face. The water felt good on her skin and it eased the hot itching of her eyelids brought on by too many hours without sleep.

She filled her hands again and drank from them. Water from a glass never tasted as sweet, she thought.

The clock chimed twice.

The night stretched before her endlessly.

Missy turned off the water and stared into her own eyes. Even in the near-dark she could see how bad she looked . . . and how old. Her skin sagged and hung in folds as loose as a hound's.

Age and gravity had collaborated on the destruction of her face.

She had been pretty once.

Abruptly she turned away; she had no time to waste on regret, and in any case, her own experience was that such feelings were futile.

She grabbed the shotgun and went back to

patrolling the house.

Standing in the living room window, she saw a police car glide silently by. It pulled to the side of the road a few yards from her drive and the lights went out.

She watched to see if anyone would get out.

No one did.

Missy stepped back from the window and wondered if, hidden by a shield of darkness, the deputy was trying to get a few minutes of sleep.

The thought infuriated her. Here she was, an old woman, staying awake all night to guard against intruders, and the police were taking catnaps. She had half a mind to call the emergency number and report him.

But no, she decided. As long as the police car was parked nearby, it would act as a deterrent. No one would be fool enough to try to break into her house with a black-and-white right out front.

With him there, maybe *she* could close her eyes and rest. . . . Ten minutes was all that she needed. Ten minutes, sitting down with her eyes closed, and she'd make it through until dawn.

Missy propped the shotgun against the wall and then tied the drapes back for an unobstructed view.

"Don't go away," she said, and hurried off to get one of the kitchen chairs, something light enough for her to carry.

The car was still there when she got back.

She settled herself into the chair with a sigh. The exertion had quickened her breathing and she put

both hands to her chest, taking comfort in the steady beat of her heart.

She let her head rest against the back of the chair and smiled at how wonderful it felt, such a simple thing. . . .

A second later, her eyelids began to droop.

Thirty-seven

Joe Ramos turned up the volume on the police radio, more from habit than anything else. At this hour, the only calls were the routine status reports on the other patrol cars. He reported his own location and then settled back in the seat.

Outside all was still, the houses dark on both sides of the street. Even the wind had died down. Another quiet night, the town living up to its name.

Pine Lane was as good a place as any to finish the few reports that were essentially the last of his duties on his final shift as a policeman. The sheriff had waived the customary two-week notice requirement, and as of 7 A.M., he would be a former cop.

That would make Rosalind and her family happy.

He wasn't sure how he felt. Admittedly, he'd been sickened by that Hightower thing . . . his first murder case. But how often would something like that happen?

Ramos shook his head. Not often at all. In fact, he

was much more likely to encounter violence in San Francisco than here. Rosalind went on and on about a "safe" job, but there were also safe places.

One murder in over twenty years, he'd heard someone say.

Sounded like a safe enough place to him. What were the priority one calls in Frisco tonight? Armed robbery, gang wars, rape, and murder? Here it was a runaway kid. A sixteen-year-old, no less.

In a big city, the police wouldn't even look for a teenaged runaway unless there was some proof that a crime had been committed. There, the streets gobbled them up and spit them out . . . sometimes dead.

Well, it was too late now; Clayton would think he was crazy if he suddenly changed his mind and asked for his job back. And Rosalind would make medical history by having kittens. . . . She'd really built up San Francisco in her mind, as if moving there would solve all their problems.

He didn't believe in magic or easy solutions.

Sighing, he flicked on the map light and reached for his clipboard. Better get started on the reports, he thought. At least he could be a good cop one last time.

The radio stayed silent.

Minutes passed. He printed carefully, mindful of how often a report would be turned back as "illegible" and have to be redone, sometimes weeks after the incident involved. Squinting in the dim light, he was so involved that it took a moment before he realized that something was moving outside.

As he turned to look, someone tapped at the passenger window.

He jumped, hand going instinctively to his gun. The face at the window gave a tentative smile.

"Shit," he swore under his breath, and opened the door to get out, "you about scared me to death."

Thirty-eight

Missy woke to the sound of a car door opening and sat forward in her chair, then had to reach out to steady herself as a wave of dizziness passed over her.

She widened her eyes and gave her head a careful shake.

What was going on out there?

The policeman had gotten out of the car and was walking around to the other side, hands held in front of him as if in supplication. She heard, faintly, the sound of his voice.

Talking to someone? But who?

Missy blinked rapidly, trying to clear the fog of sleep from her mind and eyes. She rubbed at her face, which felt somehow numb. Wake up, she directed herself.

Was there someone standing behind the car?

Yes, she could see him now. He—at least she thought it was a he—stood motionless as the deputy approached. Then he held an arm out stiffly and began to back away. The deputy stopped.

Their voices carried but she could not make out their words. If she opened the window just an inch or

two more . . .

It would make too much noise and they would know that someone was watching. Better that her presence remain unknown.

So she could only observe—like watching a movie without the sound—and wait for something to happen.

For at least ten minutes they stood talking, and then the deputy held out his hand. Hesitantly, moving stiffly, the second man walked toward him.

The deputy took the man by the arm and guided him around the car, then reached across him to open the back door.

In the manner that she'd seen in countless TV shows, the deputy attempted to help the man into the car, putting his hand on the man's head to keep him from bumping his head. . . .

In one smooth movement, the man took the gun from the deputy's holster and fired. Once. Twice.

That sound, too, was muffled.

The deputy swung backward and fell to the ground.

Missy gasped and quickly covered her mouth with her hand, involuntarily pushing back in the chair, which scraped the floor.

He looked in her direction—she saw his face clearly for the first time—and then leaned over, replacing the gun.

She closed her eyes tightly against what she did not want to see, and when she opened them, he was gone.

182

The deputy lay still.

It was a trap, she realized. If she reported what had happened, he would know she had seen, and he would come for her. He would come and nothing would stop him.

He was crazy. God help her, she had seen the insanity in his eyes.

She *could not* call for help.

Missy closed the window, locked it, and pulled the drapes. After reassuring herself that all the other windows were secured, she pushed and shoved and dragged the end tables to block the doors.

Hands shaking, she grabbed the shotgun and hurried up the stairs.

Thirty-nine

Noah knew the moment the phone rang that it wasn't good. He sat up in bed and turned on the lamp, blinking at the brightness of the light.

"Clayton," he said into the phone.

"Sheriff." McClure's voice sounded strange, as if he were choking. "Joe's been shot."

In an instant he was totally awake, his mind cleared of the last vestiges of sleep. "How bad?"

"Real bad. . . . He was alive when they found him, but just barely."

"Damn. Where is he now?"

"Still at the scene. . . . They're waiting for the ambulance."

The car slid sideways as he turned onto Pine Lane, following a few yards behind the ambulance. He accelerated out of the slide and then braked as he pulled up to the row of patrol cars parked along the side of the road.

Flashing red lights reflected off the houses and trees, and colored the grim faces of his men.

Middle of the night or not, there were the inevitable onlookers, standing silently on their porches, trying to see what they could see.

Ramos, lying motionless on the ground, was surrounded; Dr. Wyatt, a medic from the fire department, and the two ambulance attendants knelt in the dirt beside him, working feverishly to save his life.

Noah noticed the left back door of Ramos's patrol car was open, as it would be if the deputy had intended to bring someone in.

But who? McClure had been adamant in stating that Ramos had not informed dispatch of any such contact. The last radio transmission, according to the log, had been a routine "in service" at this location.

Looking into the car, he could see a clipboard on the passenger's seat, report forms fanning in the breeze from the open door. Stepping closer, he saw that the top form was only half completed.

Behind him, the sounds of activity increased, and he turned to see Ramos being lifted onto a stretcher.

For the first time, he saw the deputy's face.

It looked like his jaw had been blown away. The entire lower left side of his face had been transformed into a bloody pulp through which was detectable a white line of bone. Eyes open and glazed, Ramos appeared near death.

But when they loaded him into the ambulance, he was still breathing.

The wail of the siren faded.

"All right," Noah said, "let's get on with it. And I

186

want this one by the book."

At times like this, Noah believed, there was a kind of relief to be found in following procedure. With a minimum of talk, the investigation began.

For him, though, the next priority was notifying Ramos's wife.

At least he could tell her that Joe was alive. At least there was hope.

Hope evaporated as he turned into the driveway of the Ramos home.

The radio crackled. "All units," said the disembodied voice, "be advised . . . he didn't make it."

Noah groaned and tightened his hold on the steering wheel.

It was ironic; Rosalind Ramos had undoubtedly sent her husband off to work happily, thinking that this would be the very last time—the last long night—that she'd ever have to worry about his safety.

Now he had to be the one to tell her that, in an awful way, she was right.

She would never have to worry about Joe again.

He got out of the car and went up to the door. After taking a deep breath, he rang the bell.

At five to six he returned to the shooting site, which was by then almost deserted.

A single patrol car remained and the deputy was leaning against it, smoking a cigarette, apparently staring at the bloodstains on the ground.

It was Owen Foster. He'd been the one who'd

found Ramos after the young deputy had failed to respond to a radio check.

"Owen," Noah said, coming up beside him. "Are you about finished here?"

"Yeah . . . about. Jesus, what a mess." Foster looked at him curiously. "You told his wife?"

Noah nodded, wondering how long it would be before he would be able to forget the look in her eyes when she'd opened the door and had seen him standing there. She had known why he'd come; the wives of policemen always knew.

"Damn . . . I keep thinking, if I'd gotten here a few minutes earlier . . . driven a little faster."

"I'm not sure it would have made any difference."

"Maybe not." Foster's hand curled around the handle of his gun. "It sure would've been nice to have run into the guy who did this."

"I know how you feel, Owen, but—"

"No, don't say it." Foster knocked the ember off his cigarette and put the butt back in the pack. "I've been a cop for too many years to go and do something that stupid. Hell, I'm getting a little old to be playing vigilante. But that doesn't mean I can't think about it."

"We're all thinking about it," Noah said.

Forty

Paige eased off the accelerator as she came around the bend and saw that the road was blocked.

A police car was parked across one lane, and a wooden barricade had been put up across the other. Two men—one a uniformed officer—were standing behind the barrier, facing away from her, but they turned as she approached, and she saw that the second man was Noah Clayton. He started toward her.

Coming to a stop, she rolled down the window.

"Good morning," Clayton said.

"Sheriff." She tried to keep her voice neutral. "Is there a problem?"

He looked surprised. "There was a shooting early this morning. One of my men was killed."

Paige drew in a quick breath. "My God." She studied his face, noticing the firm set of his mouth, the resolute expression in his eyes. "I'm very sorry," she said.

Clayton nodded. "Thank you." He hesitated, placed a hand on the car door. "I want you to know that *I'm* sorry about yesterday. I'm sorry you had to

see those pictures."

"I am too." She looked away, unable or maybe just unwilling to share any more of her grief, but the anger that she'd felt had, thankfully, dissolved.

"I talked to Austin, by the way."

"Did you?"

"I think we came to an understanding. I doubt if he'll give you any more trouble."

Paige saw no point in telling him that she was considering talking to Austin herself, trouble or not.

"And," he continued, "he got those pictures from the photographer who'd taken them . . . not from anyone in the department."

"I see. Well, thank you." She glanced at him, somewhat surprised to see that it really mattered to him, that he was genuinely concerned about her problem, even while he had so much more serious problems of his own.

His smile was disarming, like that of a young boy, and she realized for the first time how attractive he was.

"Anyway"—he looked at the barricade and the smile faded—"back to business. Were you out at all last night? Did you hear anything unusual?"

Paige shook her head. "I'm sorry, I don't think I can help you. I spent the night at home, alone, and went to bed at eight. I'm still trying to catch up on last month's sleep."

"Well, that explains why you're out so early this morning."

"Actually," she said, "I have to see patients for Dr. Wyatt this morning. I'm on my way to his office now."

"Oh?" Something flickered in Clayton's eyes. "Why is that?"

"He was called out of town, rather suddenly from what I gathered."

"Really?"

"Yes, he had an emergency . . ." She stopped and frowned. "The policeman who was shot?"

Clayton did not answer, but looked to the other side of the barricade, where another car had pulled up. "I'd better let you get on your way." He withdrew his hand from the door and gave her a half-salute. "Take care."

She watched him walk away. A moment later, after pulling the barrier aside, he waved her through.

In her rearview mirror, she saw him looking after her.

A stern-faced woman opened the office door just as Paige reached for the doorknob. "You're Dr. Brown?"

She heard the challenge behind the words, saw the defiance in the woman's eyes, and sighed inwardly. "Yes," she said, and thought, not another one.

"Dr. Wyatt called to say you'd be coming in to see his morning patients." The woman, who looked painfully thin in her crisp white uniform, regarded Paige pensively. "I'm Audrey. . . . I run the office."

Paige allowed herself the tiniest of smiles, but was careful not to let the nurse see it. I'll bet you do, she thought.

"Did Dr. Wyatt tell you when he might be back?" Now that she had decided to find out what she could about her parents' deaths, she wanted to get on with

it. "I only spoke to him for a minute."

"Well, it was an *emergency*."

"So I gathered," she said, and felt a surge of impatience at the woman's officious evasiveness. "But even the most critical emergencies are over at some point in time."

"Hmm." Audrey's upper lip tightened. "I'd better show you around; the first patient'll be here soon."

"Right."

With military precision, the nurse turned and started off down the hall. Paige followed, wondering why it was that such women—strict, regimented, and humorless—seemed to gravitate to the health care field.

She had met dozens of "Audreys" over the years, rather shallow individuals who measured their self-worth in terms of their employer's importance, and who "ran the office" as if their purpose was to force compliance to an ever-changing set of rules instead of offering comfort to the ill.

"These are the examining rooms," the woman said, standing in the hall and pointing toward three open doors. "Rooms one, two, and three."

Aptly named, Paige thought, and stepped into the first room. Built-in cabinets lined two of the walls, and the counters were covered with stainless steel containers. Centered in the room was a standard padded exam table and there was a tiny dressing area in the corner behind the door. The room was saved from being totally utilitarian by a good-sized window, and sunlight flooded in through gauzy white drapes.

She reached to open a drawer and found it locked.

"I'll give you a key," Audrey said, "but make sure

192

you lock anything you open. We've had some problems with pilferage."

"Really?" For some reason, Paige never thought of a small town doctor having to deal with theft.

"Oh yes." She sniffed her disapproval. "We used to keep prescription pads in all of the rooms, and then they started disappearing. And some of the other things they take ... there are some mighty sick people around here, is all I can say, and I don't mean physically."

From somewhere in the office a phone rang, and Audrey glanced at her watch. "I'd better get that," she said, managing to sound both put-upon and benevolent, and hurried off.

Paige stuck her hands in her lab coat pockets and went to the window to look out.

Another beautiful day, she thought, and felt a pang of sorrow for the man who'd died in the night. Death always affected her more on days like this, when the sky was a deep, clear blue and the sun bathed the earth in golden warmth.

It would be very comforting to believe in an afterlife where everything could be made better.

"This life," she said softly, "this life first."

Forty-one

The phone propped against his ear, Noah leaned back in the chair and closed his eyes as he waited for a voice to come back on the line.

He had been on hold for at least five minutes, but mercifully, the coroner's office had never gone in for piping music over their phone lines. He was in no mood to be serenaded.

From beyond his closed office door he could hear the loud voices of several of the deputies, who were apparently still arguing the merits of prison versus skinning alive as a deterrent to crime. By the sound of it, prison was losing.

The shock of Ramos's death was beginning to wear off, and anger had taken its place.

Hell, he thought, they're entitled.

He'd be mad himself, if he weren't so tired.

The phone made a series of clicking sounds and a moment later he heard the harried voice of Dr. Hoskins.

"What now, Clayton?"

Noah smiled. He liked that about Hoskins; the good doctor wasted little time on interdepartmental

niceties. "What do you think?"

There was silence and then Hoskins cleared his throat. "I have to tell you, everyone here is sorry about this one. It's always harder when it's one of your own."

"It is," Noah agreed.

"You know, every so often you hear these stories about some guy coming to life just as he's about to go under the autopsy knife . . ." Hoskins coughed. "I keep hoping . . . especially with the young ones like Ramos."

Noah rubbed at the bridge of his nose. "So . . ."

"Well, he was shot twice. The first bullet entered just below the jaw on the right side, traveled upward at a slight angle, passed through the tongue, then shattered the left mandible and exited through the soft tissues of the face."

"Would that be—"

"A fatal wound? No. But the second bullet was fired at point blank range behind the right ear. It tumbled as it passed through the brain, did a lot of damage on the way. Severe damage, with hemorrhage and resultant edema. Considering all of that, it was something of a miracle that he was still alive when you got there."

"He was hanging on," Noah said, and frowned. Like a good cop.

He called the lab next.

"We're still working on Hightower and whatever you sent over on the new one hasn't even been

uncrated yet," an efficient-sounding female voice informed him.

Status quo, he thought, but said, "Can you get someone on it in a hurry?"

"I suppose I can, although from what I heard it was a contaminated scene and there probably won't be much to come out of it."

"Right, I know—"

The woman interrupted. "The victim was a cop, wasn't he?"

"Yes, and I'd appreciate your best effort."

"You got it, only don't expect anything too soon; we're backlogged with work."

"I know the feeling," he said.

Noah began to skim through the reports which had started to pile up on his desk, but found little of interest.

A door-to-door had elicited an abundance of negatives; no one would admit to having seen or heard anything. No dogs barked, no car doors slammed, and rather astonishingly, no gunshots were heard.

Apparently there were some sound sleepers on Pine Lane.

There were, however, a couple of houses where no one had answered the door, and he made a note to have a deputy try them again later in the day.

Maybe, just maybe . . .

He shook his head and tossed the reports back into the "in" basket. Then he got up and went into the

197

front office, where he dug through a stack of papers until he found what he wanted: Ramos's resignation form.

Joe Ramos had hung on to life, waiting for help to arrive so he could tell them what he knew. Only the nature of his injuries had prevented him from doing so.

He hadn't been a quitter.

Noah looked at the form and then tore it up.

Forty-two

After working in a hospital emergency department, Paige expected to find the pace of a small-town doctor's office to be slow, but thankfully, the morning was going by quickly.

And on schedule.

"Doctor doesn't make his patients wait," Audrey said pointedly, handing her an intricate chart which listed examining room availability, complaint severity, and time allocations.

The patients themselves had relatively minor complaints—sore throats, the flu, a five-year-old with an earache—and she worked steadily.

Now, as noon approached, she was anxious to finish.

"Who's next?" she asked, wondering why it was that the nurse always seemed to be lurking in the hall.

"Room three . . . is the last patient."

Paige took the chart out of the slot on the door. "Have you heard from Dr. Wyatt yet?"

"Oh yes," Audrey said, her voice conveying a smug superiority. "He informed me that he'd be in by

twelve, and he said to tell you that you needn't wait."

"Fine," Paige said. She flipped open the chart and read a brief description of the patient's complaint. Flu symptoms, but the vital signs were essentially normal. "This shouldn't take long."

Audrey sniffed. "You don't know Felicity."

Paige ignored the nurse's comment and opened the door to room three.

A young woman, her face pale and drawn, sat huddled on the examining table, the sheet wrapped tightly around her. Even at a distance, Paige could see the perspiration which had dampened the woman's reddish-blond hair.

"Hello. I'm Dr. Brown." She glanced again at the chart. "You're Felicity?"

The woman's dark eyes widened. "Oh! Yes, I—" Felicity swallowed and coughed, and her face began to color. "I am . . . I thought Dr. Wyatt . . ."

"Dr. Wyatt was called away unexpectedly." Paige smiled, hoping to put her at ease. "Now . . ." She looked at the chart again, at the nurse's notes. The patient complained of fever, headache, body aches, and malaise. "How long have you been feeling ill?"

"I woke up with it last night. I think I caught what my mother has."

For some reason, Paige noticed, the young woman looked uncomfortable.

"I see."

"Dr. Wyatt came by the house to see her yesterday, and he gave her something, I don't know what. But I think it helped. She looked better this morning." Felicity shivered and clutched the sheet to her.

200

"And you want medication?"

"I . . . I need it, you see. I can't be sick, now."

"All right," Paige said thoughtfully, and glanced again at the chart, at the nearly normal vital signs. "Let's take your temperature again."

Felicity nodded, clearly relieved.

Paige located the electronic thermometer. While waiting for the temperature to register, she studied Felicity, noting that the color had drained from the young woman's face.

As indicated in the nurse's notes, Felicity's temperature was only two-tenths of a degree above normal. No fever, but then what could account for the shivers and the sweats? Or were they psychosomatic?

She became aware that Felicity was watching her intently.

"Is it . . .?"

"You have a slight fever," Paige said, knowing that it was what the patient wanted to hear. She reached for the blood pressure cuff. "Have you been taking anything for it?"

"No. I didn't want to . . . mask my symptoms."

So there it is, Paige thought. That Felicity O'Hara understood the theory of masking symptoms showed a certain awareness of medical precepts, a sophistication generally found in patients with a tendency toward self-diagnosis and indeed, psychosomatic illnesses.

She did not comment immediately, but listened through the stethoscope to the systolic and diastolic beats; blood pressure was normal at 110 over 80.

"Well, Felicity," she said then, "you may be in the

201

early stages of a viral infection, which is difficult—"

"Can you give me a prescription for an antiviral drug?"

She might have known that was coming. "I'm not sure that's indicated at this point."

"But I can't get sick right now!" There was a desperate tone to Felicity's voice and tears glistened in her eyes. "I have to . . . I have to take care of my mother, and there are things I have to do. I . . . I just can't be sick!"

Paige repressed a sigh; it was well within Felicity's power to make herself genuinely ill. "All right, but I must warn you that the medication has only proven to be effective against Influenza A-type viruses. It may do you no good at all." She unlocked a drawer and found the prescription blanks.

"But it will, I know it will."

A few minutes later she watched Felicity O'Hara leave the office, no longer looking even the least bit ill.

Audrey, who stood waiting for her to finish the chart, sniffed disdainfully. "Cured her that quick?"

Paige felt a flash of anger, even though she'd had the same thought herself, but as she started to comment, a door opened and a well-dressed man peered out.

"Oh . . . another patient?"

"No. He's waiting for Dr. Wyatt on personal business." She took a step forward, blocking Paige's view. "I'll send the doctor straight in when he gets here. Shouldn't be long now."

202

The door closed.

Audrey turned to face her. "Excuse me, but I've got to get the rooms ready for this afternoon's patients before I go to lunch. Just leave the chart when you're finished, and be sure to lock the door behind you when you leave." With a curt nod, the nurse took off down the hall.

Paige took the chart to the reception area, leaving it and the set of keys Audrey had given her in the middle of the desk. From somewhere she heard a door opening and closing, and then the sound of men's voices, one of them Martin's.

Curious, she reentered the hall.

No one was in sight and all the doors were shut, but the voices carried.

"He's your son," Martin was saying. "You see to it."

"Damn it, I've tried, but—"

"I don't want to hear it. I'm tired of your excuses."

"It's not my fault they sent him home."

"Then send him back. That kid can bring it all crashing down on our heads."

A nasty laugh. "He's not that smart."

"He doesn't have to be smart, all he has to do is say the wrong thing in front of the wrong person . . ."

Martin's voice had gotten louder, as if he were nearing the door, and Paige stepped back around the corner just as she heard the door swing open.

"As soon as they find him, I'll send him away," the second man promised. "But it'll take—"

"I know," Martin interrupted.

They were coming in her direction, and she hurried across the waiting room, pulling the door open just enough to slide through, then closing it after her.

As beautiful as it was outside, Paige felt a definite chill as she walked quickly toward the Jaguar. Once in the car, she took a deep breath and then turned the key in the ignition.

Backing out of the parking space, she looked at the office and saw Martin staring out the window at her. In the background she could see, as well, the faces of the second man and the nurse.

Then Martin smiled and waved.

She would, she decided, go talk to Aunt Ellen after lunch.

Forty-three

Felicity stepped into the silent house and held her breath, listening for the dreaded sound of her mother's voice. Mother had been sleeping when she'd left, but all morning long she had heard the familar shrill reprimands in her mind, chastising her for her neglect.

When the words didn't come, she closed her eyes in thanks.

The air was thick and stale, and she wrinkled her nose as she headed toward her room. The house smelled like something had rotted beneath the floor.

Last summer the neighbor cat had killed a gopher, eaten its head, and left the body under the porch. There it had ripened in the heat until, gagging, she'd found it and buried it.

Thinking about the smell was enough to make the bile rise in her throat.

It was better in her room. She'd left the window open and the curtains fluttered with the breeze.

After closing the door—quietly, so her mother wouldn't hear—she went to sit at the end of the bed, opposite the window. In a minute she would go to see

if Mother needed anything, but first she needed a little time to herself.

Was that too much to ask?

"No," she said, putting her hands to her face. "I'm sick too."

Felicity opened her eyes and blinked rapidly at the brightness of the room. Her mind dulled with sleep, she struggled to sit up. She rubbed at her right arm, which had gone numb, and flexed her hand to increase blood circulation.

She hadn't meant to fall asleep.

Still massaging her arm, holding it close to her body, she got to her feet and walked unsteadily toward the door.

Once in the hall she became aware of the sharp scent of ammonia.

Was Mother doing the cleaning?

That couldn't be.

At her mother's door she stopped, leaning close to listen for a moment before raising her hand to knock.

There was no response.

"Mother?"

She took a breath, gripped the doorknob, and gave it a twist. The door creaked open.

The shades had been drawn and in the murky atmosphere of the room her eyes played tricks on her; for a heartbeat she saw death lying on the bed.

"Mother?"

The ammonia smell was stronger, and with a start she realized that her mother must have wet the bed. The covers were tangled around the older woman's

legs, but she could see dark patches where the urine had spread.

Felicity moved closer in dreadful fascination, knowing that she should be calling for help, but instead watching to see if her mother was breathing.

Which, just barely, she was. Her chest rose and fell in rapid, shallow breaths, much like, Felicity thought, a dog panting in summer heat.

"Mother? Can you hear me?"

There was no answer but Felicity saw a flutter of eyelashes and the glint of angry eyes. Two of the fingers on her mother's right hand curled inward.

That was all.

"I'll . . . I'll call someone," she said. Turning, she started toward the door, only to stop short as a thought struck her. A flurry of excitement stirred in the pit of her stomach and she felt a cold rush of adrenaline in her veins.

Did she dare?

Felicity glanced back at the bed, at the still form of her mother. A bubble of saliva had formed at one corner of the thin-lipped mouth.

Staring at that mouth, she could hear the scathing remarks which had punctuated her growing-up years. Her face warmed at the memory of seemingly endless belittlement, the pain as fresh now as it had been then.

"In a minute." Her own voice sounded strange to her, cool and collected, and very remote.

She went to the bedside table and reached for the drawer.

*　　　*　　　*

Felicity stood in a corner of the room while the ambulance attendants lifted her mother onto a stretcher.

An oxygen mask partially obscured Lenore's face, and for that Felicity was grateful. She did not wish to see the bitter accusation which she knew would be there; she had her own guilt to contend with.

But there was something else as well, something just as strong. She had, she realized, a sense of gratification, of justice long in coming.

One of the attendants tightened a leather strap across her mother's chest and then pulled a blanket up to cover her, tucking her in.

"There, now," the second attendant said, "snug as a bug."

Felicity bit her lip and lifted her chin as the first attendant turned toward her.

"Don't worry, we'll take care of your mother," he said.

Felicity nodded, not trusting her voice.

She followed them as they rolled the stretcher through the house and onto the porch, but hung back as they loaded her mother into the ambulance. Standing in the doorway, she gave a small wave.

She never would have imagined it could be so easy.

Forty-four

"Oh . . . Paige . . ." Aunt Ellen said, and took a step backward, holding the door open for her. "What a pleasant surprise."

Paige smiled apologetically. "I'm sorry I didn't call first, but—"

"Nonsense." Ellen's mouth worked at an answering smile. "Why should you? We're family, after all." She turned away. "Come . . . I was just about to have some iced tea."

Paige followed, noticing a slight hesitance in her aunt's walk, not unlike that of a drinker who suspects the ground might be moving. She wondered, fleetingly, what medication Ellen was taking for her heart.

"It's so nice out today," Ellen said when they entered the kitchen. "Shall we take our drinks outside?"

"If you'd like." She watched as her aunt poured iced tea into a tall glass and added a wedge of lemon.

"This is my favorite time of year," Ellen said, handing Paige the glass. "All the acacia blooming . . ."

Paige felt a familiar ache. "Yes," she said quietly, "I missed the acacia, living in L.A."

"It must be different . . . Los Angeles, I mean."

"It is." She sipped the tea. "Quite."

This time Ellen's smile appeared genuine, if a little sad. "You sound so much like your mother." Her voice was wistful. "Leigh was given to understatement. She was . . . almost British in that way."

"Grandmother told me much the same thing, but I don't really remember."

Ellen lowered her eyes. "No, perhaps not." She sighed. "Let's get some fresh air . . ."

Paige waited until they were settled in the shade. A breeze rippled the water which lapped against the tiled sides of the pool in a rhythmic pattern that was oddly hypnotic.

"Aunt Ellen, I wonder if you could tell me about what happened . . . to my parents."

"Oh!" Ellen glanced at her, then quickly away. "I'm . . . I'm not the one to ask."

"I don't understand."

"Of course, you wouldn't. The night it happened, I was confined to bed. In fact, it was several days before I was told, and even then, I couldn't stand to hear of it. I put my hands over my ears and refused to listen."

"But you know what happened."

"I really don't. It was so painful, I didn't *want* to know. And I had . . . other things that I . . ." her voice trailed off.

"I still don't understand."

Ellen shook her head. "I was pregnant," she said after a minute had passed. "I kept to my bed in an attempt to prevent a miscarriage, but I lost the baby anyway, soon after."

Paige reached across the table and squeezed her aunt's hand. "I'm sorry."

"Thank you." When she looked up, her eyes were wet with tears. "On days like this, when everything is so beautiful, it's hard to believe that all of that happened. Roger and Leigh, and then my baby. I keep praying it's all a bad dream, and I keep waiting to wake up."

"I know . . ."

"But even so, my loss was not as great as yours. I wish there were words to tell you, how very sorry I am. Roger was my brother, but"—a tear ran down her cheek—"losing your father, and your mother . . . in such a horrible way."

Paige, her throat tight, found she could not talk.

"I would give anything if it hadn't happened."

Paige heard anguish which matched her own, and she closed her eyes against the onslaught of memory laced with pain.

The memories came in such force that she had no defenses against them.

The two women sat for a long time without speaking.

"I remember when Roger and I were growing up, how good he was with animals. One time, when our mother cat had kittens, he managed to save three of them when they developed distemper. I remember

211

watching him feed them . . . ever so patiently. That's what kills them, you know. They can't smell the food, so they starve. He spent every cent of his allowance buying fresh fish. Roger said if they could smell anything, it would be fish." She laughed. "*He* certainly smelled like fish. But he ground the fish up and fed them, even getting up in the middle of the night so they wouldn't be too many hours without food. And he saved three of the four. The one that died . . . the distemper went to its brain. Roger cried."

Ellen raised the glass to her mouth but did not drink. "I thought he should be a veterinarian, but there was no money . . ."

"I don't know much about my father's life," Paige said. "Grandmother told me about Mother, but very little about him."

Ellen peered into the glass. "I doubt she knew much about him; she didn't altogether approve of the marriage."

"I never knew that." Troubled, Paige studied her aunt's face. "Why didn't she approve?"

"The money, I guess, or lack of it. The Chandlers were very well off . . . we were not. Leigh had a trust fund from your grandfather. I'm sure, at first, that Patrice Chandler thought Roger was out to get whatever he could."

"But that's not—"

"It wasn't true," Ellen interrupted. "My brother was a good man. An honest man."

Paige fought back a sense of outrage that anyone— Grandmother included—would think otherwise. The man who put up swings and saved kittens was

too dear to her to even consider the alternative.

Ellen went on, "Oh, she came around, after you were born. A grandchild can bring a family together when all else has failed . . . and she adored you."

"So she and my father—"

"Made their peace, yes. Of course, she established a trust fund for you independent of your parents, so you would be provided for." A frown creased Ellen's forehead. "A good thing, it turned out."

"Did Father . . . ever go to veterinarian school?"

"No, he never did."

After a while they got up to go back inside. Ellen looked tired, Paige noticed, and wondered again whether the older woman's unsteadiness was a side effect of her medication.

In the front room, Paige paused to look at the photographs on the mantel. In one of them, her parents stood alongside Martin and Ellen, who was dressed in a maternity smock. Seeing the four of them triggered a flash of memory.

"Ellen," Paige said. "I thought it was you. I thought you came and took me to your house that morning." The memory had blurred over the years. "I remember someone taking my hand and saying that we'd better go. I know it wasn't Grandmother, because she came later. But if it wasn't you, who was it?"

"I imagine it was Mrs. Sinclair."

"Who?"

"The sheriff's wife. Charlotte Sinclair."

213

Forty-five

Ellen stared into her own eyes, mesmerized by the dark emptiness of her pupils. If only she could see into that void, she might know what to do.

The right thing to do.

She turned away abruptly, and moved to the window to look out, her eyes scanning the road in both directions. She glanced at her watch. Five-nineteen.

When would Martin be home?

Restless, Ellen wandered through the house. She had been late taking her medication, and it seemed to her that every nerve in her body was charged and tingling beneath the surface of her skin.

Because of that, she had taken twice her normal dose as soon as Paige had driven away.

Any moment now, the medication would take effect.

Ellen stopped by the mantel, picking up the photograph that she had seen Paige studying. Roger smiled widely into the camera, his dark eyes—gray,

like his daughter's—conveying satisfaction with his life.

"I've got everything I ever wanted," Roger had told her. "And I want you to have what you want, too."

"I will," she had replied, her hands moving protectively to her abdomen. "Soon."

"Are you sure?" He leaned forward, placing his hands over hers. "Are you certain this is the right thing to do? I mean, Martin has two more years—"

Ellen shook her head stubbornly. "We'll manage. We've got a little money put aside, and I know how to get by. That's been our entire lives, Roger . . . getting by."

"I know you do. Hell, I've seen you make one chicken last through a week's worth of meals, but this is different."

"I don't see how."

Roger sighed. "Martin's not like us. He didn't come up the same way. He doesn't like to sacrifice . . ."

"He won't have to. I'll—"

"You'll what? Pretend you've eaten already, and give him your dinner? You're pregnant, Elly. You can't be pulling Mama's tricks."

"There are other ways."

Roger's eyes were sad. "Even if there are, it won't be enough. How much have you got saved?"

Ellen felt her face redden, and thought for a moment that she just wouldn't answer. But she and Roger had been through too many hard times, and she knew he was on her side.

"About two months' pay."

His mouth twisted. "And it'll take five months or longer before you can go back to work."

"I'll . . . we'll manage."

Roger was silent as he got up from the kitchen table and walked over to look out the window. With his back to her, he asked, "Is Martin as happy about this as you are?"

"You know he isn't," she said as calmly as she could. "But after the baby is born he'll change his mind. We'll be a family, the way you and Mama and I were . . ."

"Elly, you're dreaming."

"I'm not!"

He laughed, but it was a kind laugh, and he turned to meet her eyes. "You can't hold a marriage together with a baby."

"It's not like that," she protested.

"Then how is it? Why can't you wait to start a family until Martin sets up his practice? Why the hurry?"

"Oh, but you and Leigh—"

"Yes, we had Paige before we were really ready, but the circumstances were not the same."

"Because she has money." Even as she said the words, Ellen wanted to take them back.

"There's that," he conceded, "but even without it, we were on solid ground."

Ellen averted her eyes. "Martin loves me."

Roger crossed the room and squatted in front of her, taking both of her hands in his. "I'm not saying that he doesn't, but you know . . . he doesn't act like a happy man."

"He works too hard. He hardly ever sleeps. It won't always be this way."

"Elly, listen to me." He squeezed her hands. "Listen. I know the look in Martin's eyes. I know it, and you know it, too. He's feeling trapped, Elly, closed in. Whether it's the work, or the baby, or not having any money . . . it doesn't matter. If something doesn't give . . ."

She shook her head. "He won't leave me. He loves me."

"I know he does. But under pressure—"

"*I'll* handle the pressure."

Roger lifted her hand to his mouth and kissed it, "Lord love you, you can't do it all."

"I can. And I will. If I have to beg in the—" Tears blurred her vision and a sob rose in her throat. "I want this baby. Nobody understands."

"I'm trying to."

"I want Martin, and I want this baby." She wiped at her face with a trembling hand.

Roger stroked her hair. "If it was my money, I'd give it to you," he said. "If it was my money . . ."

If it was my money.

Ellen turned to see the front door open.

"Ellen," Martin said, "why are you standing here in the dark?"

"I've always been," she whispered.

Forty-six

Cody waited for his eyes to adjust to the dark.

The night was still and blessedly cool, and he felt better than he had all day. His headache, courtesy of Sheriff Noah Clayton, was finally gone. The pills—courtesy of a feel-good doctor in L.A.—had managed only to dull the edge of pain that sliced through his head. It had been one of the worst . . . and the first in months.

The first, in fact, since he'd begun work on the book.

He took a deep breath, filling his lungs with the cool, fresh air.

He'd spent the day inside, reviewing his notes, staying out of sight, and hoping that the old adage was true and that he'd be out of mind as well—Clayton's mind. The last thing he needed, at this stage of the game, was the attention of the local police. Although from what he'd heard from Mrs. Sinclair, the police had their hands full.

There was a murderer in town. Rather, another murderer, this one a cop killer.

A cop getting killed tended to stir things up; he

wondered if Clayton would sleep tonight. If anyone would sleep tonight.

Stepping off the porch, he started walking toward town.

Only one car had gone by in the fifteen minutes since he'd left the house. The female driver, her face pale and drawn, had rolled up the window as she passed, staring at him with saucer eyes, apparently afraid that he would leap at her and drag her from her car.

Irrational fear was one of the side effects of murder, but perhaps she was right to be wary. Death could come so quickly, without warning, often without reason.

That was what made it so fascinating.

He had always been curious: How would it feel to look into a murderer's eyes and know that time had run out?

How did it feel to die?

And how did it feel to kill?

He shivered, acutely aware of the stillness around him. He wasn't afraid, but walking along the dark side of the road, it was hard to ignore the feeling that he was being watched, that somewhere beyond the trees, someone was keeping track of his movements.

As he had kept track of others . . .

It would be ironic, he thought, if, having come to put an end to a twenty-six-year-old mystery, he got caught up in another.

*   *   *

When he reached the town, he found the stores and offices closed, and the sound of his footsteps echoed eerily as he walked the empty streets.

Looking ahead, he watched a patrol car pull away from in front of the city building. It made a tight U-turn and then accelerated, heading away from him.

From where he stood he could see a second patrol car parked in the shadows across from the library. The glowing tip of a cigarette was the only indication that someone was inside.

Cody smiled faintly.

The police were on duty; the streets were safe tonight.

Forty-seven

Noah saw them in the sweep of his headlights and shook his head in disbelief. He hit the siren, allowing it to begin its wail and then turned it off. Switching on the emergency lights, he steered into the parking lot.

Three faces looked in his direction and one man—Otis Carter—began to wave.

He pulled up alongside the front of the building and got out of the car.

"Sheriff," Carter said, his voice slurred, "good of you to come by."

"What are you guys doing here?" He looked past them to the door of the tavern, and saw that the police padlock was still in place.

"Where else would we be?"

"Home."

"Shit, Noah, I was home last night," Fred Ellis said. "My wife can only stand so much of my company." He was a big man with the florid complexion of a steady drinker, and known to get louder with each shot. He had a reputation as a mean drunk.

223

"Well, I sympathize with her, but the tavern's closed."

"Noooo." Ellis held up a bottle and peered at the contents. "Not closed yet."

Carter reached for the bottle. "I'll help you close up . . ."

"Hard to drink with a busted arm," Ellis said, his eyes reflecting the red of the revolving lights.

"All right." Noah stepped between them. "Let's keep it friendly, or I might have cause to remember the old drunk-in-public statute."

Ellis grinned and flung his thick arm around Carter's shoulders. "We're all friends here, Noah, just mourning a fallen buddy . . ."

"Buddy . . . Bucky . . . our buddy Bucky." Mitch Stuart sat on the steps, elbows propped on his knees, holding his head between his hands. "Who . . . who played Bucky . . . or was it Buddy . . . on 'The Dick Van Dyke Show'?"

Noah frowned. "I think Mitch's had enough mourning for one night."

"That's good . . . mourning at night." Ellis's mouth held a hard-lined smile. "We're not bothering anybody."

"I believe you," Noah said, glancing from face to face. With the exception of Ellis, no one looked like trouble. "But somebody might bother you. There's been two men killed in the past few days."

For a moment nobody spoke, and then Mitch lurched unsteadily to his feet.

"Morey Amsterdam," he hiccuped.

"Hell, Mitch," Carter complained, "you shouldn't answer your own questions."

224

"See?" Ellis winked. "Just a couple of good ole boys having a good ole time. No harm in that, is there?"

Noah hooked his thumbs in his belt and shifted his weight onto his heels. "I think, for your own safety, all of you'd better go home."

Ellis took a swig from the bottle. "We're safe . . ." he said, "there's three of us. . . . Only a fool would go up against three men at once."

Noah smiled and curled his hand around his night stick. "A fool or a man with a gun."

"What year . . ." Mitch said, "did 'Have Gun, Will Travel,' get canceled?"

"Who the fuck cares?" Carter said, throwing his hands in the air.

"Richard Boone . . . and it was 1963."

Carter turned to Noah. "Make him stop answering his own questions."

Noah regarded all of them. They were not, he suspected, as drunk as they appeared to be. He'd caught a few warning looks passing between them, and Carter seemed downright anxious about something.

"Maybe he could answer some of mine." Facing Mitch, he nonetheless detected the studied blankness of the other two men's expressions, the classic 'know-nothing' look. "Mitch . . . were you here Saturday night?"

"Here?" The slack-jawed grin had faded.

"At the tavern. The night Hightower was killed."

"Well, yeah."

"And you, Otis?"

Carter smiled hesitantly and looked at Ellis before

answering. "You know I was. This is the only place in town."

"Fred?"

"Sure, I was here for a while." There was no bluster in the big man now. "Left before midnight, though. . . . My wife can tell you that."

"That'll be easy to verify, then." He glanced benignly at Carter. "But you closed the place that night, right Otis?"

"I guess you know I did."

Noah nodded but didn't comment, content to let Carter stew on it. "Was there any trouble?"

"No, no trouble. Or at least, I didn't see any."

"How did Bucky seem to you?"

Again, that quick exchange of looks.

"Just Bucky." Carter reached for the bottle Ellis held, and Ellis surrendered it without protest. "You know how he could be, Noah."

"I know. Like a rattlesnake with its tail caught under a rock—liable to strike out at anything in reach." He paused. "How was he on Saturday?"

"Jumpy . . . on edge," Carter admitted. "Kept waving around that cannon of his, like he was Dirty Harry or something. Said anyone who wanted to mess with him could step right up."

Noah tried to reconcile that with the way Hightower had tried to downplay the skunk incident as an isolated event. "Did he say anything about who he thought wanted to mess with him?"

Ellis's big hand landed on Carter's shoulder and gave him a little shake. "Everybody from his third grade teacher to the IRS." His laugh seemed forced. "Everybody except for his mother, and I'd bet he had

his doubts about her."

"Did he name any names?" Noah looked at Mitch, who was leaning against a post, hands clasped across his stomach. "How about it, Mitch?"

"I didn't hear any names." He swallowed noisily and drew a hand across his mouth.

"What did you hear?"

"All I heard him say was . . . the baker."

"Who?"

Mitch grimaced and shook his head. "The baker. The guy who gave him his bread."

That sounded like Bucky, Noah thought. "Meaning money?"

"I don't know. I don't know." He made a move forward and waved his arm toward Ellis and Carter. "Ask them . . . I gotta puke."

Noah watched Mitch stagger off and then turned to the others. "Well?"

"I don't—" Ellis began.

"The game is over," Noah interrupted, suddenly annoyed. "If you know anything, you'd better tell me now, because if I find out later, I'll charge you with withholding evidence, and whatever else I can think of."

"Shit. I don't really know—"

"Neither of us do," Carter cut in.

"The only thing I heard from Bucky is that he was getting his money from somebody." There was nothing drunk about Ellis now. "He liked to bellyache about business, but the truth was, he didn't give a damn, because he was skimming the gravy off somebody else's plate."

"Who? Do you have any idea?"

Ellis shrugged. "He never said."

"Otis?"

"Someone in town."

"What makes you say that?"

Carter cleared his throat. "A couple of years ago, back when Naomi left him, he came by my place, drunker than I'd ever seen him. Said he had a meeting with a business associate. I told him, 'Hell, Bucky, you ain't got no associates.' And then he told me . . .'"

"Go on," Noah prompted.

"Somebody was paying him off for something he knew."

"Blackmail?"

"I guess. I didn't ask. I thought . . . I thought he was making it up."

"What made you change your mind?"

"A day or two later, we were in the bar," he said, indicating Mitch and Ellis, "and we saw the money."

"A lot of money," Ellis added.

"We come to find out that he got regular payments . . . deliveries, he called them. Every six months or so."

"When you say you came to find out, what do you mean?"

The guarded look reappeared on their faces. Ellis, he saw, had begun to sweat, the perspiration shining red in the light from the patrol car. From a distance came the sound of retching. Judging by Carter's sick expression, he might be next.

"We followed him."

"You followed him."

"We weren't going to rip him off, or anything," Carter hastened to add. "We just—"

228

"Were curious." Noah had to work to keep the skepticism out of his voice.

"Yeah, we were. So . . ." A shaky grin. "He drove up to Hillcrest Road."

Noah frowned. "Pretty deserted up there."

"We had to stay back, because of the dust. . . . I mean, if he looked in his rearview mirror, he would've seen us if we got too close."

"And?"

"We sort of lost him. He must've turned onto one of those trails that branch off the road. We went all the way to the end of Hillcrest . . . didn't see him."

"So how do you know—"

Ellis answered, "We went back down and waited for him."

"And you're sure he was there to get money?"

"If you'd seen his face, you'd know he had." Carter looked to Ellis for confirmation.

"Did you see anyone else?"

Both men shook their heads. "Nope. And we waited until it got dark. Whoever it was got there before we did, and left after we were gone."

Noah didn't like the turn the case was taking. Instead of answers, he had managed only to uncover more pieces to the puzzle.

"Do you," he said, "have any suspicions as to who it might have been?"

"I wish I did," Ellis said fervently. "If I knew, I'd put the touch on them myself."

Noah believed that.

He watched as Carter and Ellis manhandled Mitch

into the back of Carter's red Cadillac. A moment later their taillights disappeared into the dark.

He got into the patrol car and switched off the lights.

In the silence, he found himself wondering if there was another way, a back way, down from Hillcrest Road.

WEDNESDAY

Forty-eight

Stephen hung from the branch for a moment before dropping to the ground. He patted his pockets, reassuring himself that the apples he'd picked were still there, then moved away from the road and toward the covering darkness of the woods.

It would not be dark much longer, he knew; the moon was going down, and to the east, the black of night was giving way to the dawn.

He would sleep when the sun came.

He'd found a safe place, not far from where, as a boy, he'd found the leather man. A hollowed tree, with just enough room for him to curl up inside.

Stephen walked carefully, keeping his eyes on the ground and trying not to let the sharp fragrance of the apples drive him to hurry. His stomach grumbled, but he'd almost gotten used to being hungry, and he did his best to ignore it.

He stepped lightly, but even so he was accompanied by the occasional snapping of twigs. All he could do was hope that no one listened.

Although he hadn't seen anyone in many hours,

and only once had he heard the motor of a car, he'd learned well that some—like the leather man—had cloaks to hide behind, cloaks which shielded them from being seen as they watched. . . .

Ahead he saw his hiding place and he stuck his hand in his pocket, feeling the slightly rough skin of the apple beneath his trembling fingers. His mouth began to water and he swallowed repeatedly.

He took a final look around and then ducked into the dark center of the tree.

The apples were hard and tart, but he ate hungrily, gnawing and chewing the fruit until all that was left was a small pile of cores. Those he eyed thoughtfully for a moment before picking one up and popping it into his mouth.

He did not know how long it would be before he would eat again.

When he'd finished he licked at his hands and sucked his fingers to clean them. Some of the apple had gotten under his fingernails—along with the dirt—and he scraped each nail between his teeth, chewing what was dislodged.

Now he needed water.

There were no houses nearby, but people liked to dump things along the road, and he'd seen an old cracked porcelain sink among the weeds. Even a broken sink could hold water, if it was angled right. All he needed was a mouthful.

Only . . . daylight was near.

Stephen ran his tongue over his lips, but even as he

imagined himself drinking the water, how it would taste, how it would feel going down his dry throat, he knew he'd have to wait.

They were looking for him.

If they found him, he would be punished for what he'd done.

Forty-nine

Missy opened her eyes to the light of day, vaguely surprised to find herself still among the living.

Or what passed for it.

She had fallen asleep in the rocking chair by the bedroom window, and a dull ache radiated from her lower back up into her ribcage. Taking a firm hold on the chair to steady herself, she lurched to her feet.

Assorted pangs and twinges competed for her attention, but she had no patience for the harbingers of age, and when her step faltered, she determinedly went on.

At the window Missy parted the curtains and looked down to where, the night before last, the policeman had been shot. There was little indication that anything of significance had taken place, only a rust-colored stain on the ground.

Had the man died?

Missy hestitated, looking down the stairway toward the front door.

Yesterday morning, someone had come knocking.

Shotgun loaded and in hand, she'd waited for them to try and break in, but after a few minutes she heard footsteps going away.

They had come back once since then, just before dusk, and they would, she suspected, return again.

What did they want from her?

She had nothing to tell them.

Missy started downstairs. By the time she was halfway, she began to feel dizzy, and she realized that she'd been holding her breath.

"Nothing but foolishness," she said out loud, but in her heart she didn't feel it. There was good reason to be cautious: the destruction of her garden now seemed a portent of worse things to come.

Before going into the kitchen, she checked the locks on the front door.

She stabbed the fork into a chunk of carrot and lifted it daintily from the can. Tapping the fork on the edge of the can, she waited until the brown sauce—gravy?—finished dripping, and then bit into the somewhat mushy vegetable.

Stew, they called it, but it was no kin to the hearty fare she'd grown up eating and now cooked herself. The potatoes, beneath the pseudo-gravy, looked gray and mealy. Chunks of meat reminded her of the dog food she'd seen advertised on TV.

"Never had a dog," she whispered, "but if I did, I wouldn't feed him this."

Maybe it tasted better warmed. She frowned and glanced toward the oven.

But no, if she heated the stew, it would surely give off a smell, and anyone lurking about outside would

know that she was in the house. Cooking smells were a dead giveaway.

Missy peered into the can and felt a sudden loss of appetite. Her mouth tasted oily and stale. Disgusted, she tossed the can in the garbage and put the fork in the sink, lining it up with the others she'd used since . . . when? Monday, was it?

A long time ago.

She took a glass and went to the refrigerator. Jars of water filled every shelf; the plumbing made the most god-awful noise and she didn't want anyone to hear the water running. She grabbed the nearest jar. . . .

It slipped through her fingers and crashed to the floor.

For an instant she could only stand there, watching as trails of water snaked out in all directions, diverted here and there by large pieces of glass.

Then she felt the sting of a score of tiny cuts on her legs.

Dark red blood began to well. Diluted with water, it ran down her shins and soaked into the cloth of her slippers.

Missy stared, fascinated in spite of the giddy feeling it gave her to look at her own blood. She could hear the *whoosh* of her pulse in her ears, and knew she was near fainting. Her vision clouded, but somehow she managed to make her way to the front room, where she went to her knees abruptly, and then lay on the floor.

Try as she might, she could not keep her eyes open.

In the background, she thought she heard, or maybe imagined, someone pounding on her door.

Fifty

Paige cut the engine, pushed in the clutch, and allowed the Jaguar to coast to a stop in front of the Sinclair house. It was a big house, almost antebellum in style, with columns on either side of the massive wood door.

She glanced at her watch. Eight-thirty. She hadn't called for an appointment, but was fairly certain Charlotte Sinclair would be home.

Paige did not want to bother Mrs. Sinclair, but she herself had been up most of the night, sleeping only fitfully. When she had slept, her dreams were full of possible revelations, the most disturbing of which involved a secret door into a room where her parents were preserved under a Plexiglas dome.

Someday she'd ask Alex what it meant.

As she started up the porch steps, the front door was flung open, and a heavyset woman rushed out. The woman was dressed in an immaculate gray linen pantsuit, accentuated with ropes of pearls. Her auburn hair was arranged into a mass of regimented curls which looked as if they might be able to withstand a nuclear explosion.

241

"Oh! You're not the carpenter," the woman said.

"No I'm not. . . . Are you Mrs. Sinclair?"

The woman's eyebrows came together in concentration. "I am, but, do I know you?"

"From years ago, Mrs. Sinclair. I'm Paige Brown."

"Oh!" She frowned. "My goodness, I would never have recognized you," she said, and clasped her hands primly in front of her.

"I wanted to talk to you. Have I come at a bad time?"

"No, not a bad time, exactly, but . . ."

Paige waited for her to continue.

". . . not a good time, either. The carpenter is coming today, and I've so much to do before I leave."

"It'll only take a few minutes."

"Yes, well, I suppose I . . ." One hand went to her plump throat. "You'd better come in."

Paige hadn't known what to expect of Charlotte Sinclair, but the grim tone of the woman's voice had caught her off-guard. She followed behind and tried to imagine what was the cause of the older woman's unease.

Walking down a narrow hall, she noticed that portholes—identical to those found on a ship—lined both walls along the way. Oddly shaped red clay pots hung from macrame holders, but there were no plants in them.

They went into a large room, which at first glance appeared to open onto a patio, but then Paige saw that the lush greenery was merely painted on the wall. There were, in fact, no windows in the outer walls.

With some surprise, she looked at her hostess.

Charlotte Sinclair had perched on a workman's stool and she motioned to Paige to do the same.

"I'm sorry there are no chairs, but with the remodeling—"

"This is fine."

"One day, I'll have it finished. Of course, it'd be done by now, if I stayed home more, but I find that hard to do." She laughed shrilly.

Paige glanced around the room. Aware that Mrs. Sinclair was watching her, she nodded toward the mural. "Interesting."

"Isn't it? Franklin would have hated it, but"—she averted her eyes—"it's *my* house now. One mustn't be afraid to make a statement, in how one chooses to live." She stared absently at the wall.

"Mrs. Sinclair, I wonder if I might ask you a few questions?"

The older woman looked uncomfortable, but nodded. "I assume this is about your family?"

"It is. My aunt tells me that you were the one who took me away that morning."

"That's true. Ellen had been confined to bed, so I was the logical choice, being the sheriff's wife." Her expression softened. "You were a lovely child . . . no trouble at all."

Paige hesitated. "There's so little I remember. I know my grandmother came for me, but I don't know when."

"Oh, several days passed before her arrival. Three days, if memory serves."

"Three days." Paige struggled to remember. "Did I . . . say anything to you about what happened?"

"Not a word, and that was the way I wanted it.

Franklin thought I should question you—you wouldn't talk to him or any of the others—but you'd been through enough. Surprised Franklin when I stood up to him . . ." Her smile was rueful. "Surprised myself more."

"So I didn't talk to the . . . to Mr. Sinclair?"

Charlotte shook her head. "You hardly said a word the entire time you were with us. Then your grandmother came. *She* was a woman to be reckoned with; Franklin wanted you to go back to the house and see if anything came to mind, but she backed him down. Scolded him, she did, for trying to get a child to do his work for him."

Paige smiled, thinking of how often she'd seen Grandmother take charge of a given situation. Patrice Chandler had been an irresistible force who'd never met an unmovable object.

"She brought a lawyer with her, and in a matter of hours, she'd gotten custody, and that was that."

"Can you tell me, Mrs. Sinclair, what happened then?"

"You mean, after you left Tranquility?"

"Yes."

The frown returned. "It's been a very long time."

"Whatever you can recall." Hoping to prod the woman's memory, she asked, "They never arrested anyone, did they?"

"No." Charlotte pursed her lips and tilted her head, as if something had just occurred to her. "Although I remember Franklin talking about bringing someone in."

Paige felt a surge of excitement. "Who, do you know?"

244

"Oh, no, just someone passing through . . . a drifter. He'd been put off a train down in Leland. He hung around town for a couple of days. I never heard what came of it."

"Is there anyone who might know?"

Charlotte fingered a strand of pearls. "You might ask Martin," she suggested hesitantly.

"Martin Wyatt?"

"Well, yes. He was a big help to Franklin, I can tell you that, although I thought he'd be better off at home with his wife. And then she lost the baby . . ."

"He helped with the investigation?"

A quick nod. "Franklin even commented that it was a shame that Martin hadn't gone into law . . . said he had a fine mind for the kind of detail involved."

"That's interesting." Aunt Ellen had never told her about any of this.

"And your Uncle Martin was Franklin's biggest supporter when my husband decided to go to law school."

"I see." She didn't, but she forced a smile anyway. "Well, thank you for your help."

"Not at all," Charlotte Sinclair said. "After all, in a town this size, aren't we all family?"

Paige wondered.

Fifty-one

Felicity leaned forward and stared out the car window, her hands—which were clenched into tight fists—tucked beneath the folds of her skirt. The seat belt was snug across her right shoulder, binding her in.

"Relax, we're almost there," Dr. Wyatt said.

She nodded quickly, to prove that she was listening, and had been listening all the way from Leland and the hospital. "Yes, thank you." And although there was no point, she added, "I could have taken the bus home."

"Nonsense."

Felicity heard the casual dismissal in his voice, the tone adults used when speaking to foolish children whose ideas were too silly for consideration. But she was not a child and the word stung . . . especially coming from him.

"Your mother will be all right," he said, glancing in her direction.

She stifled an urge to laugh.

"Guillain-Barré is rarely fatal once the acute episode is past."

"I know," she said softly.

Dr. Wyatt apparently did not hear. "Her recovery may take a while . . . with the therapy and all, and she'll need to be in the hospital until she's stable. But she'll be home before you know it."

The car slowed as they neared the outskirts of town. The sight of familiar buildings eased the tightness in Felicity's chest. She made herself sit back in the seat. Soon, she thought.

"If you'd like, you could stay the night with us."

Surprised, she turned to look at him for the first time since they'd left the hospital. "What?"

He kept his eyes on the road. "It must be . . . lonely . . . in that house all by yourself."

Felicity knew better than to answer truthfully, knew better than to tell him that the house had always been lonely, whether or not she was alone. So she didn't answer at all.

"Ellen could use the company; she doesn't get out much these days. And I'd feel better knowing someone was there with her."

"I can't." She looked away, embarrassed by the sharpness of her voice.

If he was taken aback, he gave no sign. "Well, if you change your mind . . ."

Felicity stood at the front window and waited for the doctor to drive off. He had remained parked at the curb in the big car, its powerful engine idling, while she'd let herself into the house. There was no reason for him not to leave, but the car did not move.

Was he watching from behind the tinted glass?

248

The thought made her jumpy.

"What do you want from me?" she asked.

A second later, the car pulled away. For a time she remained at the window, to reassure herself that he would not come back.

Then, feeling foolish, she forced herself to abandon her watch.

Dr. Wyatt had been their family doctor for as long as she could remember. Some of her earliest memories were of sitting in an examining room, waiting for him to come in and make her feel better.

His hands were always cool and his touch was gentle. He smelled of soap, a special kind of soap that only doctors used. There was comfort in that smell.

When she was very young, he would pick her up when he came in the room, and hold her while he talked to her mother. She could remember laying her head on his shoulder, against the starched fabric of his white coat. It, too, was cool.

More than once, feeling safe, she had fallen asleep in his arms.

She'd hated it when she got too big to be held.

Why was she afraid of him now?

But she *knew* why.

The journals were still where she'd hidden them, in the hall closet, along with the leather satchel. She'd not had time to look through them, but now, with the house to herself, she would satisfy her curiosity.

Arms full, she went into the front room and stopped short, her heart thudding painfully.

The front door stood open.

Hadn't she locked the door? Maddeningly, it was one memory that escaped her, and she tried to visualize what had happened after she'd come in. Had she gone straight to the window to watch Dr. Wyatt leave? Had she, this time, forgotten to lock the . . .

From within the house, she heard a creaking sound.

Feeling panic rise in her throat, she rushed toward the door. A little off-balance from the weight in her arms and from the satchel, which banged against her thigh, she hurried outside. She ducked around the corner of the house and hid behind the bushes, wincing as something sharp snagged her hair and scraped the back of her neck.

She huddled there, eyes closed, and tried not to hear the rasping sound of her own breathing.

Felicity wanted to be able to hear him as he came near. . . .

"No one's after me."

The certainty of the words was not reflected in the tone of her voice, which sounded choked and tremulous, like an old woman's. She didn't like that voice.

"He's gone," Felicity said, much louder than she had intended. She tightened her arms around the journals and pressed her back against the rough wall behind her. "I'm safe," she whispered, "I'm safe."

When no one reached through the bushes to grab her, she breathed a sigh of relief.

A moment later she was walking rapidly down the street. A quick look over her shoulder and she saw that the front door—which she had definitely left open—was now closed.

Someone had been in the house.

Felicity would not go back until the journals were in a safe place . . . and she knew just where to take them.

Fifty-two

"The funeral's tomorrow."

Noah's grip tightened on the pencil, but he finished writing before looking up.

McClure frowned at him from the doorway.

"That soon?"

"I gather that the widow is anxious to get away from here." There was an undercurrent of bitterness in McClure's tone. "From what her father told me, she doesn't want all the—and I quote—'police jazz' complicating her life."

Noah found he was not surprised. Even in the early moments of shock and grief, after he'd told her of Joe's death, he'd been aware of an accusatory look in Rosalind's eyes. But given the circumstances, it was understandable that she blamed the police for her husband's murder.

"It'll be all right," Noah said. "We have to respect her wishes."

"Joe deserves better." McClure turned and walked away.

Noah understood his agitation; in the brotherhood of policemen, it was traditional that a fallen officer

be laid to rest with honor. That included the attendance—in full dress uniform—of officers from surrounding areas, a twenty-one-gun salute, and when it could be arranged, a fly-by in the "missing man" formation favored by the military.

With the funeral scheduled for tomorrow, there would be no time to pull it all together. . . .

Noah answered the phone on the first ring. "Clayton."

"Sheriff, I thought of something. What you were asking about last night."

He recognized Mitch Stuart's voice, sounding none the worse for wear, and felt a sense of wonder at the man's capacity, to say nothing of his recuperative powers. "Tell me, Mitch."

"You asked how Bucky was acting that night, and I've been thinking about it. There was something else that was bothering him, other than that skunk business."

"Go on."

"Well, I don't know what time it was or anything, but it was after dark. Bucky went to take the trash out, and when he came back in, I could tell he was pissed off about something. His face was red and he was cussing a mile a minute." Mitch lowered his voice. "Not your everyday cussing either. I mean, this was the serious stuff."

Noah glanced up; a clerk from records had come into the office with a stack of manila folders which she put on top of the pile in the "in" basket. He waited for her to leave before asking, "Did he say

what he was mad about?"

"Yes and no. First he was ranting that people were no better than animals, and it would be a good thing if some of the dumber ones were, you know, fixed. So they couldn't breed. Then he said something about putting the little fuckers to sleep."

"Serious stuff," Noah agreed, making notes on a pad.

"I got to tell you, I was confused. . . . I'd had a few drinks by then, and he was talking so fast, it was hard to follow. I think Otis finally asked him what the hell he was talking about, and Bucky says, 'You got puppies you don't want, you drown 'em.' I said, 'Hey, I'd like a puppy,' and then he laughed, kind of nasty. Told me to go out back, there was a mongrel out there digging through his trash."

Noah frowned. "Is there more?"

"He didn't *say* any more, but a little later I had to, you know, use the facilities, and I took a look out the back door, It was dark out, like I said, but I could just make him out . . ."

"Him?"

"A kid. There was a kid scrounging through the garbage cans."

"Did you recognize him?"

A hesitation. "No. He had blond hair, though. Looked to be maybe fourteen or so."

Noah reached for the stack of folders, pulling the pile toward him. Beneath them was the report on Stephen Goldstein, who was sixteen but looked younger, and had hair blond enough to be seen in the dark.

"It about made me sick," Mitch went on. "The kid

255

was standing there and I guess he was hungry, because he was eating stuff that he pulled out of the garbage."

Mitch continued to talk, but Noah had stopped listening, hearing instead the voice of the doctor at the private hospital where the boy had been a patient: *"I don't think Stevie is dangerous."*

"Mitch," Noah interrupted, studying the photograph of Stephen which Horace Goldstein had grudgingly supplied, "can you come down to the office and take a look at a picture for me? See if you can ID the kid?"

"I suppose I could, but I'd have to close up the shop, and I'd hate to have to do that. . . . Most of my customers come in on their lunch hours."

Mitch owned a television repair business about a block away from City Hall. Noah considered offering to take the photograph there, but decided against it. Three walls of the shop were lined with television sets, about half of which were playing at any given time. It was nearly impossible to concentrate amid the racket, and the flashing screens always seemed to distract Mitch, who had been known to give back more in change than he'd received in payment if what he saw excited him enough.

Noah did not want to trust an ID made under those circumstances. "How about later this afternoon then?" He glanced at his watch: nearly one.

"Sure enough."

Noah hung up the phone and looked again at the photograph.

The boy's features were even and sharply defined, and there was nothing of the . . . slackness . . . that he'd often observed in the faces of the mentally ill.

But the eyes, he thought, the eyes. Empty and dull, they stared at him with the death-fogged gaze of a corpse. No light, no awareness.

It was as though the boy were dead.

A preliminary report had come from the crime scene lab, indicating, as he'd suspected, that there was nothing of evidential value at the site of Ramos's shooting.

All that had shown up was a good quantity of blood and bits and pieces of the wrappings of medical supplies.

The scene had been "contaminated," as the analyst had said yesterday, by their efforts to save Joe's life. The medics—and probably everyone else who'd been there—had inadvertently destroyed whatever microscopic clues might have been left by the killer.

Based on the theory that whomever was at the crime scene both took something and left something behind, it was possible, even likely, that whatever the murderer had left had then been borne away on the shoes or clothing of those who'd sought to help his victim.

Evidence or not, preservation of life had to come first, and if by trying to save Joe they'd also given his assailant a break . . . so be it.

It was too bad that they had no physical evidence, but Noah knew there were other ways to catch a killer.

Thinking of that, he wondered if anyone had ever gotten ahold of Missy Prentice.

Fifty-three

The bleeding had stopped.

With trembling fingers, Missy plucked at the slivers of glass which pierced her skin, trying not to push any of the splinters deeper. Her hands were sticky, her own blood dried and caked beneath her fingernails.

Looking at her wounds, she felt a sense of outrage at the circumstances which had led to this. . . .

She had no doubt that all of it was connected. Everything that had happened in the past few days, she was certain, was part of a madman's plan.

Why had she been singled out?

That question, the same question she kept coming back to, time and time again, flashed through her mind, accompanied by a confusion of images. As if glimpsed in half-light, faces moved in quick succession before her eyes, eluding her attempts to put names to them.

One of them, its mouth wide and gaping, seemed to stretch lengthwise until it resembled a rubber mask, the features contorted into a grimace of agony.

She shook her head to clear it; there was no time to

waste on fanciful thoughts.

Now, more than ever, she felt vulnerable to further attack.

But she would be ready for them when they came for her.

The shotgun tucked under her arm, Missy began to make her way slowly up the stairs.

Even moving slowly, she had to struggle to breathe, and she felt a dull ache in her chest. A sudden wave of nausea threatened her equilibrium and—frightened that she might faint again—she eased herself down into a sitting position.

Sweat trickled down her back, and when she brushed her hand across her forehead, it came away wet.

Missy propped the shotgun against the banister and then leaned forward, cradling her head in her hands. Her skin felt cool and clammy to the touch. . . . She wiped at her face with the hem of her dress.

For a moment she could only sit, the damp fabric pressed to her face, trying to catch her breath.

"Oh Lord," she whispered, and was startled to hear the oxygen-starved rasp of her own voice, sounding very much like a death rattle.

It frightened her.

But slowly her breathing eased, and the pressure in her chest lessened. She began to feel stronger.

Looking down the stairs, she saw that she had an unobstructed view of the front door.

This would be as good a place as any to wait it out.

Fifty-four

Paige recognized Martin's car in the lot in front of his office. The office was closed today, she knew, but there was a second car, and she wondered if her uncle had come to meet a patient or . . . someone else.

She parked between the two cars.

Putting her hand on the hood to gauge how much heat the engine was giving off, she concluded that Martin hadn't just arrived. The engine of the second car was pinging.

Paige walked to the office door and cautiously tried the doorknob. It was locked.

Leaning her head closer to the door, she strained to hear voices from inside, but the only sound was a low-pitched hum that might have been the air conditioner.

Aware all at once of what her actions would look like to someone passing by, she raised her hand to knock. When there was no answer after a minute, she rapped harder, and then took a step back as the door swung open.

"Oh," Audrey said, clearly surprised. She was dressed in jeans and a thin sweater, and without the

protective camouflage of her uniform she seemed less than intimidating.

Paige smiled. "Hello Audrey. Is Dr. Wyatt in?"

Color stained the woman's cheeks as she glanced over Paige's shoulder, apparently at Martin's car. "Well, yes, he is, but"—she blinked—"he's not seeing patients."

"I'm not a patient." Paige stepped inside. It was dark and cool, and from somewhere a radio played calypso music. "Working overtime?" she asked.

Audrey had closed the door and now leaned against it. "I often come in when the office is closed," she stammered. "It's the best time to catch up on my work . . . with the service answering the phones."

"How commendable." She gestured toward the back. "Is Martin in his office?"

Audrey nodded, one hand going to her throat. She was, Paige noticed, wearing vamp-red fingernail polish.

Martin looked up as she entered the inner office. "Paige!" He'd been seated on the small couch opposite his desk, and he got to his feet a little clumsily. The top three buttons of his white shirt were undone, and his jacket and tie were thrown across the top of a wood filing cabinet. "I wasn't expecting—"

"I need to talk to you." The music died out and for a moment there was absolute silence. "If it's convenient?"

"Certainly, no problem. I was catching up on some work, but it's nothing that can't wait." He

crossed to the door and shut it, then turned to face her, one hand casually rebuttoning his shirt. "What's on your mind?"

"Did Aunt Ellen tell you I talked to her yesterday?"

Martin shook his head. "No, she didn't mention it, but she wasn't feeling too well when I got home. She went to bed early. Why?"

"I thought she might have talked to you about it." She took a breath before continuing. "I've decided that I want to know more about what happened to my parents."

"That's understandable." He sat on a corner of his desk. "I don't know how much Ellen can help you, though. She was pretty much out of things . . ."

"Yes, she told me. I was sorry to hear about the baby."

Martin sighed, looked away. "It may have been for the best."

"How so?"

"Ellen was never . . . strong. Even as a young woman, she suffered from one ailment after another. If she'd had a child, I wonder if it mightn't have weakened her, even . . ." he hesitated, his voice lowering, "killed her."

"I wouldn't think—"

Martin interrupted, "You don't know your aunt. She can be obsessive. It would have been very much like her to neglect her own health in favor of her baby's. Not getting enough sleep, not eating, running herself ragged trying to be the perfect mother." He sounded bitter, but he smiled and shrugged. "She wanted to adopt you, after . . . but your grandmother wouldn't hear of it."

263

That was a surprise. "Really?"

"That summer, after she'd recovered from . . . everything . . . she went down to Los Angeles to try and convince Mrs. Chandler that we would be good parents for you. Ellen thought, considering your grandmother's age, that she'd find it difficult to have a young child in the house."

Paige searched her memory, but she did not recall having Aunt Ellen as a guest in the big house. Grandmother had brought her back to Tranquility for a visit that first summer—which had been when Paige gathered the acacia blossoms for her parents' graves—but otherwise . . .

"Needless to say, your grandmother had her way." Martin straightened his shirt cuffs. "And it all worked out for the best in the long run."

Paige knew she was getting sidetracked, but she had to ask. "Why didn't you and Aunt Ellen adopt another child? If she was that desperate to have one?"

"I don't think she was desperate to have *a* child. She wanted one of her own, and you—as her brother's daughter—qualified." He shook his head. "When she finally accepted that Patrice wasn't going to hand you over, she just put aside all thoughts of motherhood."

"And what about you?"

The question apparently caught him by surprise. She noted a quick flash of annoyance in his eyes.

"To be honest," he said dryly, "it never mattered much to me. A lot of men feel that way."

Thinking of her own father, Paige did not agree, but there was little to be gained by challenging his statement. "Did Aunt Ellen know how you felt?"

"We never talked about it."

Paige remembered her aunt's anguished face and wondered at the quality of a marriage where husband and wife neglected to talk about what mattered in their lives.

Pointedly, Martin looked at his watch.

"I also spoke to Charlotte Sinclair," she said.

"Charlotte? I thought she was off on one of her cruises." He reached across the desk, picked up a stack of envelopes, and began to shuffle through them.

"She told me that you were very helpful to the sheriff after my parents' deaths."

The shuffling slowed and he peered at one envelope for a long moment before glancing up at her. "Everyone in town did what they could to help," he said finally. "In a small town like this, people tend to draw together when something bad happens."

Paige considered him for a moment before continuing. His expression was friendly and open, as if he had nothing to hide. Why, then, did she believe otherwise?

"I wondered, why you never mentioned it to me."

His eyebrows arched. "At the time? You were eight years old, Paige."

"But I'm not eight anymore . . ."

"Granted, but I'd come to the conclusion that you didn't want to know. The times I've seen you since then . . . you never talked about it."

That was true, but she wasn't willing to let it go at that. "You could've told me."

"No, Paige, I couldn't. You've forgotten how *closed* you were about all of this. To tell you the

truth, I was surprised when Ellen told me you were coming here. I thought you'd gotten past what happened here."

"How could I get past it? They were my . . ." She stopped and swallowed hard. "They were my parents."

There was a long silence. If Audrey was still in the office, she was being very quiet.

Martin cleared his throat. "There isn't much I can tell you, anyway. I was only here for four weeks before I had to return to my residency . . . and after that I only came home for weekends."

"Mrs. Sinclair told me that they picked a man up for questioning."

"Ah . . . yes, that's true."

"Were you here then? Do you know what happened to him?"

"I was here," Martin said slowly, "but I wasn't involved in that particular episode." He folded his arms across his chest.

"But you must've heard."

"There was certainly talk, but I dismissed most of it as just that—talk."

She regarded him curiously. "What kind of talk?"

"Oh, what you'd expect . . . that they'd put the fear of God into him. I gather they were a little heavy-handed, roughed him up some."

"Who were *they?*"

"Sinclair—"

"The sheriff?" she interrupted. "The sheriff was involved in roughing up a suspect?"

"Feelings were running high." He shrugged, and then got to his feet, walking over to the window to

look out. "Anyway, nothing came of it, as far as I know. They let him go."

Something about his offhand manner bothered her. "When you say nothing came of it, what do you mean?"

"Well, that's a presumption on my part, since, as I said, they let the man go."

"And after that?"

"Things quieted down. Frank went on investigating, but if he found another suspect, I never . . ."

Voices could be heard from the hallway, and they both looked toward the door.

"Excuse me," Martin said, striding across the room. He opened the door to reveal Audrey's startled face. Behind her stood a uniformed policeman.

"Dr. Wyatt," the officer said, stepping in front of Audrey, who seemed incapable of speech. "I wonder if you would come along with me."

Fifty-five

Noah adjusted the volume of the radio, but static largely obscured the dispatcher's voice. Seventeen years of listening to police broadcasts enabled him to decipher the message: Foster was en route with Dr. Wyatt.

He got out of the patrol car and stared at the Prentice house, wondering if the old woman were laying dead in one of the rooms.

No one had seen her since Monday, according to the neighbors, who now stood on their lawns, apparently waiting to see if their quiet street had once again been visited by death. He noticed Austin was there, standing slightly behind and to one side of the others.

Noah had already circled the house, trying the doors, but everything was locked tight. They'd have to break in.

He glanced up at the sky. Clouds had appeared to the west—the weather report called for rain by morning—but it was still warm, and it would be, in all probability, much warmer inside the house. If Missy had gone to meet her maker, there was a

distinct possibility that the body had ripened.

The radio crackled again and he heard Foster's voice announce he'd arrived at the scene. Noah turned and saw the patrol car turn onto Pine Lane, followed closely by a silver Jaguar. Paige Brown's car.

A low murmur of excitement came from those watching.

Wyatt was the first one out, medical bag in hand. "Sheriff," he said, "what's—"

Noah held up his hand. "In a minute." He looked past the doctor to Foster. "She's got dead bolts on both doors. Do you have a crowbar?"

"Sure," Foster nodded.

Paige Brown came up to stand beside her uncle. "Is there anything I can do to help?"

Noah was acutely aware of her gray eyes studying him, and of the delicate scent of her perfume. "You can stand by . . ."

"Your deputy said this was a medical assist." Wyatt pivoted to glance at the small group across the way, then looked toward the house. "Is she ill?"

"I don't know. She may be ill, she might have injured herself, or she may be dead. But given that no one's seen her in more than forty-eight hours, I want a doctor on hand when we go in."

Foster came up to them, a three-foot crowbar in his hands. "This'll do it."

Noah nodded. "All right . . ." He found himself looking at Paige. "Let's get it over with."

The front door was heavy, made of solid wood, and

270

it resisted their efforts to pry it open. Ten minutes of trying, and all they had to show for it were a couple of gouges in the wood.

Foster, sweat streaming down his face, lowered the crowbar and whistled in amazement.

"Son-of-a-bitch door."

"How about the back?" Wyatt suggested.

Noah and Foster exchanged glances. "What do you think?"

Foster kicked at the door, which didn't even rattle in its frame. "Take a tank to get through this. It must be fucking mahogany . . . excuse me, ma'am."

Noah took a step back, looking at the windows. It would be easier by far to crack one of them and just climb in. "Let's try something else."

"I'm for that." Foster wiped his forehead with the back of his hand. "They're a little high off the ground, though."

"I'll give you a boost." He paused, looking at the bushes which grew close to the building. Whatever her motives for planting thorny bushes around her house, Missy had made the place into something of a fortress. It would not be easy to get through them. "Shit."

"The back?"

"I don't think we have a choice," Noah conceded.

The chisel end of the crowbar dug into the wood like a warm knife through butter.

"There we go," Foster said.

There was a splintering sound and chips of wood flew outward, along with half of the dead bolt, which

landed at Paige's feet.

"Something's blocking it." Foster sounded exasperated.

Noah stepped closer, put his hand in the middle of the door, and shoved. The door moved about a quarter of an inch. "What the hell?"

"She's got junk piled against the door."

Noah turned to Wyatt, who stood, grim-faced, at the bottom of the steps. "Would you give us a hand?"

It took all three of them to push the door open wide enough to get through. Noah went in, standing just inside and blocking the others. Glass crunched beneath his boots and he kicked aside a large piece, watching as it spun across the floor. Boxes were stacked three deep behind the door, and he wondered who or what Missy was barricading out.

He sniffed. The house smelled stale, unlived in, but there was not, thank God, the putrid stench of death.

He motioned the doctor to come inside.

"I'll check upstairs," Wyatt said, moving past him.

"Right . . ." The door to the basement was open, and he gestured toward it. "Owen, why don't you look down there?"

Foster nodded and disappeared into the darkness.

Paige stood beside the splintered door. "Can I help?"

His eyes were drawn to her throat, watching the play of muscle as she spoke. "No, you'd better—"

The blast shook the house.

In the split second before he could move, it came again, the booming sound of a shotgun.

Fifty-six

Blood was splattered all over the floor, all over the walls.

Paige kneeled beside her uncle where he lay in the hall, and tried to assess the extent of his injuries. She felt for a carotid pulse, found it, and glanced at his face.

His eyes were open but glassy, his skin ashen.

She pulled at his shirt, which clung to him wetly, damp with bright red blood, and popped the buttons in her hurry to open it.

His chest was peppered with wounds. A shotgun, then, with the shot dispersion pattern indicating that he hadn't been hit at close range. Still, she knew from her experience in emergency that, even when fired from a distance, the pellets could do a great deal of damage.

She was vaguely aware of the movements of the others in the room, of the old woman's gibbering protests as they led her away, but Paige did not look up.

"His bag," she said urgently.

Someone handed her the black leather medical

bag. She held her breath as she opened it, afraid that it might well contain only the rudimentary items which a country doctor would need. . . .

A small, 250-milliliter container of 5 percent dextrose in water was nestled in one corner of the bag. Next to the IV fluid was intravenous tubing, a three-way stopcock, and an 18-gauge intracath needle.

Two hundred and fifty wasn't much, but it was better than nothing, she thought. She ripped open the packaging.

"An ambulance is on the way." Noah Clayton squatted beside her. "How is he?"

"Not good." She found a tourniquet, tied it around her uncle's upper arm. "How long will it take the ambulance to get here?"

"Ten, fifteen minutes."

"Damn." Locating the vein, she deftly inserted the needle. "I want you to send someone to get medical supplies from his office." She connected the tubing to the needle and then taped it in place.

"Just tell me what you need."

Paige looked at Martin's face. His eyes were closed, now, but he breathed unevenly through parted lips. "A miracle."

He was still alive when the ambulance arrived, his color improved. She'd managed to stablize his heartbeat—which had been approaching tachycardia—with medication, but it was still touch and go.

Paige stood back for a moment, watching as the medics moved him onto a stretcher. The floor where he'd been laying was slick with blood.

"Wait a minute," she said, and reached to untangle the intravenous line, which had gotten wrapped around the cardiac monitoring equipment.

"Are you riding along?" a medic asked.

"Yes." She turned to the sheriff. "Will you notify my aunt?"

He nodded. "I'll go over there myself."

"Please be careful. . . . She has a heart condition." Paige frowned, looking after her uncle as he was carried out of the house. "You might want to wait until you can get another ambulance to stand by . . ."

"All right."

Paige started out the door and then hesitated, looking back at him. "What happened here?"

Clayton shook his head. "I don't know, but," he said, his eyes grim, "I'll find out."

Sitting on the fold-down seat across from the stretcher, Paige braced herself for the ride down to Leland and the hospital.

From inside the ambulance, the siren sounded distant and unreal.

She leaned forward and placed the stethoscope on her patient's chest. He was breathing rapidly, lungs straining, and she adjusted the oxygen flow to the nasal cannula. The cardiac monitor indicated a few premature ventricular contractions, but he had essentially a normal sinus rhythm.

"How's the doc?" The medic had positioned himself at the foot of the stretcher and was filling out the inevitable paperwork.

Paige thought for a moment before answering

275

"All things considered, I'd say he's doing okay." Almost unconsciously she looked at her watch, trying to estimate how much of the so-called "golden hour" afforded to saving trauma patients still remained. He would have to be rushed into surgery. . . .

Thinking of that, she asked, "Did you notify the hospital that he's going to need transfusing?"

"Absolutely. He was a donor to the blood bank, so they've got his blood type and subtype on record."

"Good, we're going to—" she began, when the ambulance swerved suddenly and she had to grab onto an overhead railing to keep from falling. From the corner of her eye she saw the outraged face of a motorist as the ambulance cut in front of him. A horn blared.

"Idiot," the medic said.

"—need every break we can get."

The surgical team was ready for them when they arrived. In a flurry of activity, the nurses prepped Martin for OR while she gave a brief history to the surgeon.

"I'd like to stand in, if you don't mind," she said when she'd finished.

The surgeon, a slightly built young Korean, nodded solemnly. "If you wish." His eyes examined her blood-stained clothes. "It will take many hours. There are"—he looked back at the x-rays—"many, many wounds."

Fifty-seven

Clouds obscured the sunset.

A wind had come up, cooling things off, and now the air smelled of rain.

From his position across the road, Cody watched as a deputy put a police seal on the front door.

They had taken the old woman away right after the ambulance left. A deputy on either side of her, she'd been hustled into the backseat of a patrol car as whispers of excitement rippled through the growing crowd.

While everyone else was pushing forward to get a better look at her, he'd crossed to where Paige Brown's Jaguar was parked, nonchalantly reaching in through the open window and extracting the keys.

No one had noticed.

Now, with the house locked up and the last police car pulling off, people began to drift away, walking slowly back toward their houses, still speculating about what had happened.

The police, as always, were very close-mouthed.

Cody glanced at the sky. He'd wait until dark and then come back for the car.

Until then . . .

His fingers closed around the key chain; he'd start by going through her house.

He went upstairs to the bedroom. Pushing the door open, he hesitated, then decided against turning on the lights. It would make things more difficult, working in the dark, with only the thin beam of his penlight, but he'd done it before.

Lights on or off, it was an art to toss a room without leaving things out of place, and he was grateful that he'd been taught by a master.

"Take your time," Priestly used to say. "Get a feel for this room before you start searching. And know what you're looking for."

Cody smiled to himself.

What he was looking for would not be found hidden in a drawer or under a box spring or tucked between the pages of a book. It would not be in a safe deposit box at a bank, or wrapped in foil and frozen beneath the ice cube tray in the freezer.

What he was truly after existed only in the mind of Paige Seaton Brown.

What he wanted were her memories.

But . . . to get to them, he had to get to her. And if he was perceptive enough, he might learn enough about her, in this room, to make that not only possible, but inevitable.

It was fully dark when he finished, or rather, gave up.

She eluded him, perhaps because she'd been in the

house for only a few days. Or maybe she had gotten so good at hiding that she did it without conscious effort.

He closed the door gently.

Downstairs, he was startled by a light which shone through the front room windows. He felt a pulse of pain begin in his temples from the sudden brightness, and he put up a hand to shield his eyes.

The light shifted, moved away and back again.

He heard, then, the idling of a car engine, and narrowing his eyes, he could make out the distinctive markings and silhouette of a police car. The cop had trained a spotlight on the house.

Cody stayed perfectly still, knowing that, at a distance, he would not be detectable unless he moved.

Was it Clayton?

The light died, but the patrol car stayed put.

He pressed the button on the side of his watch: nine-twelve. If the cop didn't leave soon, he would have to sneak out and take the roundabout way back to town.

And the longer he was delayed, the more likely his plans would be thwarted.

"Come *on*," he said under his breath. He could see a shadowy form inside the car, imagined that he could see a face looking in his direction. His head throbbed.

The car inched forward, stopped.

He closed his eyes. Was the cop playing with him? Had he been seen? He fought an impulse to run.

When he opened his eyes, the patrol car had gone.

The Jaguar started on the first turn of the key, its

powerful engine running smoothly.

Cody waited, but no porch lights came on, nor did he see a face at any window. With two shootings having taken place in the neighborhood such a short time apart, he half expected someone to challenge him.

He adjusted the mirrors, catching a glimpse of his face. The headache was gone, but it had left him looking drawn and tired, and there was a tightness around his eyes.

A quick stop at the cottage would fix him up. A few pills . . .

He put the car into gear and pulled away slowly.

In his hurry, he didn't see them, and he stumbled, grabbing onto the door frame to keep from falling.

Someone had placed a stack of thin books—old-style account books—in front of his door.

He picked one up, opening it to the first page.

November 9th, 1961: Frank has announced his resignation, but we all knew it was coming. Why shouldn't he resign? Now that he has all that money . . . and so little sense.

Cody flipped through the pages, all filled with the same precise handwriting. Whose handwriting was it, he wondered, but it didn't really matter.

April 12th, 1962: Oh, how the mighty have fallen! After all his talk about opening a practice in San Francisco, Martin has "changed

his mind." Or was it changed for him?

He bent down to pick up the rest of the books, gathering them in his arms like treasure.

It was unfortunate that he hadn't time to read them now, but he couldn't keep the lady waiting.

Fifty-eight

Noah made it back to Tranquility just before midnight.

His headlights cut through the silent, deserted streets, and he slowed, acutely aware of feelings of isolation brought on by the blackness of the night.

Beneath the cover of darkness, anyone could hide.

He swung into the paved lot beside City Hall and parked in the mayor's slot.

Switching off the motor, he sat for a moment, listening to the crickets and the call of a night bird. The wind had come up and it rustled through the branches of the trees.

The sounds soothed him.

It had been a long day.

Noah frowned, thinking of Ellen Wyatt.

She hadn't said a word, just stared at him as he'd told her what had happened. The color left her face so quickly that it seemed an optical illusion. She stepped backward, started to turn away, and then slumped to the floor.

"She's only fainted," the medic said after listening to her heart.

Nonetheless, she was taken away by ambulance to the hospital where her husband was undergoing emergency surgery. Within an hour of her admission, she suffered an apparent heart attack, and was, the last he'd heard, in guarded condition in the cardiac care unit.

The word on Martin Wyatt was equally as grim: the surgeon estimated that Wyatt had a less than even chance at survival. They were still in the operating room when he'd stopped by the hospital at 9 P.M., more than seven hours after the shooting, and surgery was expected to continue into the early hours of the morning.

And then there was Missy Prentice. After the shooting, she'd become more and more disoriented, rambling on about her garden and a class assignment which was due on Monday without exception. Her gaze was unfocused, and she blinked repeatedly. A tremor shook her frail body.

Fearing that she might be near collapse, he'd had her taken to the locked ward at the county hospital in Leland. The doctor who'd admitted her felt she was in a dissociative state. She could not, the doctor said, answer any questions.

Three victims of one senseless act.

He got out of the patrol car, locked it, and then crossed toward the building.

The work had piled up on his desk.

Noah unbuttoned the top button of his shirt with one hand as he shuffled through the reports, looking for Mitch Stuart's statement. A lab report on the .44

magnum they'd found in Hightower's car indicated that the gun had not been fired in the recent past. A second report stated that the rod used in the killing was made of a common metal alloy, but was unidentifiable as to origin.

"Great," he said.

When he found Stuart's statement, he skimmed the page. It was pretty much what he'd expected: Mitch had positively identified Stephen Goldstein as the boy he'd seen digging through the trash behind the tavern.

So . . . he had an ID. By itself, it didn't mean much, and proved nothing.

Still, Bucky had died a scant few hours after an altercation with the boy. Although Hoskins had said that it would've taken the strength of an adult male to inflict the fatal wound—and the Goldstein boy was of slender build—Noah thought Stephen was a likely suspect.

Add that to the boy's questionable mental health and the fact that he had run away and was presumably hiding out. . . .

A very likely suspect, Noah thought.

After notifying dispatch to issue an "approach with caution" warning pertaining to Stephen Goldstein, he tried to reach Paige Brown at the hospital.

"She's still in surgery, Sheriff," the night supervisor informed him.

"Still?" He glanced at his watch; it was 12:30 A.M. "It's been—"

"Over ten hours," she interrupted. "But I think

they're about finished.''

"How's the patient?''

"I can't really say, except that he's made it through thus far.''

"How about Ellen Wyatt? Do you know her condition?''

The sound of a beeper came clearly across the line. "Hold on,'' the woman said.

He heard a garbled voice followed by a blast of static.

"I'm sorry, but they're coming out of OR and I've got to get over there.''

"Listen,'' Noah said hurriedly, afraid she would hang up. "Be sure to give Dr. Brown my message and have her call—''

"Yes, yes, I will.''

A click and then the line went dead.

He looked at the receiver and wondered whether he should call back. It wasn't that he didn't believe the nursing supervisor's assurances that she would give Paige his message; it was just that he knew how often messages went astray.

And he didn't want her to learn about her aunt's illness through someone's careless remark.

On the other hand, she *was* a doctor and she was in her own element. After the shooting, she'd been calm and in control, and he had no cause to think that she wouldn't handle Ellen's hospitalization in the same, cool manner.

Paige Brown, he decided, could take any crisis that came her way.

THURSDAY

Fifty-nine

Paige stood aside as the nurses and technicians pushed the gurney and life support equipment through the double doors into the OR antechamber. The "beep" of the cardiac monitor echoed eerily as they moved into the dimly lit hall.

"Dr. Brown," someone said, and when she turned, a nurse thrust a piece of paper into her hand before hurrying off after the others.

She watched the entourage go through the second set of doors.

"He is doing well," Dr. Park said, coming up beside her. Sweat ringed the neck of his greens and his hair was plastered to his head.

She nodded. "Thank you." The surgery had been flawless; Park was a meticulous surgeon, as good as any doctor she'd ever observed.

"The danger now is from infection, but I think he will be fine." Dr. Park smiled and inclined his head. "And how will you be?"

"I'll be fine," Paige said, and wondered if that were true.

"I tell you . . . sometimes, I worry more about the

family than the patient. I want him to sleep, he sleeps. But"—he shook his head—"the family is not so easy. You should go home, now, get some rest."

"I will." She closed her fingers around the message the nurse had given her and tucked it into the pocket of her greens. "As soon as I make a few phone calls."

Paige leaned back in the chair and ran a hand through her hair, listening to the phone ring. No answer. Had Aunt Ellen come down to the hospital? Most likely, she thought.

She tapped the switch hook, breaking the connection, and then dialed the operator, who answered on the first ring.

"Operator."

"This is Dr. Brown." Paige spoke softly, although she was alone in the doctor's lounge. "I need to locate the family of Martin Wyatt. Would you ring the waiting room for me?"

"Oh, there's no one in the waiting room, Doctor. It's right across from me, and there's nobody there."

"I see. Is there an ICU waiting room?"

"Yes, but there's no one there either. It's kept locked at night, and I've got the key right here on my board."

Paige frowned. "Is there any way to verify whether someone . . . a visitor . . . is in the hospital?"

"Well, I'm not allowed to page at night . . ." the operator began.

"Perhaps she went to the cafeteria for coffee. Is there a phone in there?"

"Yes, I can ring the cafeteria, if you'd like. Who is

it you're looking for?"

"Ellen Wyatt."

"Hmm. The name's familiar."

"She may have—"

"Oh, wait! Oh." The woman's voice changed, became grave. "I have an Ellen Wyatt who was admitted to CCU this evening."

"Oh God." Paige closed her eyes.

"Dr. Brown? Can I connect you to CCU?"

It took an effort to answer. "No, I'll . . . I'll go on up." She hung up and took a deep breath to steady herself. The exhaustion she'd been holding at bay all evening swept upon her with sudden force.

What next? she wondered. Ellen and Martin were all the family she had left.

God never gives you more than you can bear. It was Grandmother's favorite saying. *You'll be as strong as you need to be.*

Paige covered her face with her hands.

She could not help thinking that God—and Grandmother—had overestimated her.

From the hall came the sound of voices and quiet laughter.

Paige raised her head, wiped at the tears beneath her eyes and got slowly to her feet. She went into the restroom to splash cold water on her face, avoiding her reflection in the mirror.

She did not want to see the look in her eyes.

After drying her hands and face, she crossed through the lounge and went out into the hall which was again deserted.

She saw no one on the way to CCU.

"The admitting diagnosis was myocardial infarction with ventricular tachycardia," the charge nurse informed her, leading her to the bedside. "The emergency room physician successfully converted the V-tach using electrical shock and lidocaine." She spoke in hushed tones. "Potassium chloride was also given after the blood chemistry showed a low serum potassium level."

Although Paige knew very well what to expect, it was still something of a shock to see Ellen lying motionless amid the monitors and machinery native to Coronary Care. The respirator hissed rhythmically.

"How is she?"

"She's listed as critical," the nurse answered. She pulled the curtains around the bed—the CCU equivalent of privacy—and then disappeared between them.

Paige squeezed her aunt's hand, but there was no answering pressure.

Standing there, looking upon her aunt's pale face, Paige felt strangely numb.

In a way, that was a relief.

She stayed until a nurse came to draw blood for the early morning lab work.

She took the elevator down to the ground floor.

Walking down the hall, Paige was momentarily overcome by a wave of dizziness, and she had to lean against a wall for support while waiting for it to pass.

She took several deep breaths, careful not to hyperventilate.

The smooth surface of the wall felt cool against her face, the way, she thought wistfully, that clean sheets feel on a summer night.

"Dr. Brown? You are all right?"

Her eyes were slow to open. Dr. Park, dressed now in an immaculate linen suit, stood a few feet away. He watched her with mild curiosity.

She straightened. "I'm fine, just a little tired." She glanced at her watch and was surprised to see that it was almost four-thirty.

Park nodded politely and looked at his own watch. "I think I must go home before it is time for me to begin rounds. You, also?"

"No . . . I'm on vacation," she said with a weary smile.

"An unusual vacation," Park observed. He smiled, nodded again, then turned away. A moment later he went through the double doors at the end of the hall and a rush of fresh air swept in.

Paige realized that she hadn't asked him about Martin, and she hurried after him.

Mercury vapor lamps lit the parking area but she didn't see where Dr. Park had gone. Dressed still in OR greens, she shivered as she looked around. She rubbed her bare arms and rotated slowly, scanning the rows of cars.

From her left she heard a car door opening and she turned in that direction.

The car, she saw with surprise, was her own.

Cody Austin stood beside it.

Sixty

"What the hell are you doing back here?"

Noah didn't break stride. "Work to do."

"Well," McClure called after him, "you'll be much more efficient with, what? Two hours of sleep?"

Noah unlocked his office door and gave it a kick. He was not in the best of moods; he hadn't slept at all.

The paperwork on his desk looked as if it might have multiplied while he was gone, and he resisted an impulse to sweep it to the floor.

"Want coffee?" McClure asked from the doorway. Noah shook his head. "Thanks, but I'm running on pure adrenaline." He sat down at the desk and reached for a stack of file folders. Opening the first folder, he stared blankly at the field information form and tried to concentrate.

"Since you're here, you might as well have a look at these." McClure handed him two more folders and, not waiting for a response, turned and left the room.

One was a report from a resident of Pine Lane who had—two days after the fact—suddenly recalled hearing men's voices outside on the night Joe Ramos

was killed. But because it was so late and he didn't want to disturb his wife, he hadn't bothered to get up and look to see who was talking or what was going on. He still insisted that he hadn't heard the shots.

Furthermore, within the text of his statement, the man offered his opinion that it was just a coincidence; he was certain that the voices had nothing to do with the shooting. He had reached that conclusion because, while he hadn't been able to hear all of the conversation, what he *had* heard seemed innocuous. Neither man sounded angry, and one of them had offered the other a ride home, and even something to eat.

Noah blinked and sat up straight. A ride home? Something to eat?

"Damn," he swore softly, putting it all together and not much liking what he saw.

Joe had to have been talking to a runaway; it was the only thing that made sense. No cop would offer food to someone he didn't think really needed to eat. And on that particular night, the someone had to be, could only be, Stephen Goldstein.

Ramos must have tried to befriend the boy. And it had cost him his life.

What had the psychiatrist said? *I don't think Stevie is dangerous.*

"Little Stevie is a killer," Noah said aloud.

After issuing a second alert on the Goldstein boy, Noah, oddly restless, decided to go out on patrol. The storekeeper had said that his boy preferred the night, and there was perhaps an hour left before sunrise.

The kid was hiding somewhere.

Dark clouds hung low in the sky, threatening to keep morning at bay, and the wind had the smell of rain in it as it lashed at his face.

As he pulled away, the first big drops of rain splattered on the windshield.

Sixty-one

The sweet tartness of strawberry Jell-O, eaten dry from the box, made the muscles in Stephen's jaw ache, but it tasted too good to stop.

He licked his fingers—already stained pink—and pressed them into the sugary granules, then stuck them in his mouth. The texture pleased him and he slid his tongue back and forth over his fingertips as he sucked.

The strawberry smell filled the narrow confines of the tree.

There had been a picnic, when he'd been in school, and one of the mothers had made Dixie cups full of strawberry Jell-O with bananas sliced into it. A tiny dab of whipped cream had topped it off, and he'd traded his corn chips for a second cup.

Tipping his head back, he poured some of the Jell-O into his mouth.

It made him want to sneeze.

Stephen rubbed at his nose and then reached for the paper bag to see what else there was, if there was anything else to eat. He up-ended the bag.

A tin of brown shoe polish, a can of condensed

milk, and a box of kitchen matches.

Stephen picked up the milk and hefted it. After studying the can for a minute, he decided that he would find a sharp stick, a flat rock, and punch a hole in it.

Putting the can down, he reached for the matches.

Sixty-two

"It's really coming down," Cody said.

Paige stared out the rain-sheeted window, watching the road ahead of them. The wipers beat rhythmically, lulling her into a half-trance.

She rolled down the side window an inch or so, letting the air cool her. The smell of wet pavement reminded her of when she was a child, when she would rush outside and run down to the road after a storm to breathe in the freshness left behind by the rain clouds.

And how the sun would come out, and the pavement would steam . . .

And the windows in the kitchen would be fogged over because always, *always*, her mother cooked soup on those days.

Paige closed her eyes, felt an icy sting as droplets of rain blew into her face.

It had rained that day.

Paige sat at the kitchen table, blowing on her soup and swinging her legs under the chair.

"Be still," her mother said, but didn't turn from the stove.

Paige sighed and hooked her stockinged feet on the chair rungs. Her socks were damp and the toes had begun to sag and droop. She reached with one hand and tugged on the right sock, pulling it up.

"Mama, can I have some crackers?"

"In a minute."

Paige twisted in the chair. "I can get them. I can reach them."

"Just a minute, I said."

Something in her mother's voice told her not to argue. "When is Daddy coming home?"

"He should be home now, but he's not, is he?"

Paige frowned, straightened in the chair, and picked up her spoon. She had heard them last night, their raised, angry voices finding the way to her ears, even though she had pulled the covers over her head. She swirled figure eights in the soup.

Her mother came to sit at the table, but Paige did not look up from her bowl.

"Oh," her mother said, getting back up again and crossing to the cupboard. "I forgot your crackers."

Paige swallowed the first spoonful of soup. "It's all right, I don't need them." She smiled tentatively at her mother. "It's good without crackers."

Mother turned, the box in her hands. The corners of her mouth twitched, but her smile, if it was a smile, faded half-formed. "Just in case." She put the box of crackers on the table in front of Paige.

Paige looked at it and then at her mother. She didn't know what to say.

Neither of them spoke.

Paige ate as quietly as she could, swallowing the small chunks of vegetables whole rather than chewing them. She was careful not to clank the spoon against the side of the bowl. Because her mother had gotten them, she took a few crackers and laid them on the table beside her bowl.

A few minutes later she heard the sound of her father's truck pull up outside.

She looked at her mother from beneath her eyelashes.

Father's footsteps approached the kitchen and the door swung open. "Oh no," he said, pulling off his rain slicker, "I'm late for lunch again."

"It's on the stove."

Paige glanced quickly from one to the other, and then spooned the last drops of soup into her mouth. She put her hand over the crackers and, after making sure neither of them were watching, tucked them in the folds of her napkin.

Her father leaned down and kissed the top of her head, then ruffled her hair. "Hi, sweetie."

She smiled at him shyly, glad that *he* wasn't angry with her. "Daddy."

"Paige, if you're finished . . ."

She nodded and slid sideways out of the chair. Without being told, she took her bowl and rinsed it in the sink.

Silence followed her out of the kitchen.

Once in her room she went straight to her hobby horse, and started to rock slowly. Her legs were longer than when she'd gotten the horse, but she braced her feet on the wooden pegs anyway, and ignored the awkward position of her knees.

It was only quiet for a little while, and then she heard them, fighting.

She was scared and angry, and she didn't understand.

She wanted them to stop.

Paige lowered her face into the shelter of her arms and started to cry.

She became aware that the car had stopped and she opened her eyes. They were, she was surprised to see, at the house.

"Are you all right?"

A hand squeezed hers, warm and comforting, and she turned to find him watching her.

Cody placed his hand gently against her face.

For a moment she couldn't answer, could only look into the smoky blue of his eyes.

Rain pounded the roof of the car.

He leaned toward her and his hand moved to cup the back of her head, pulling her forward, closer to him.

His mouth lightly brushed hers, and she felt a wave of pleasure flow through her. She took a deep breath and made herself back away.

He did not try to stop her.

The rain let up just then, and she got out of the car and ran to the house, then had to wait for him to follow and give her the keys. She took the key ring, fumbled with the lock, and pushed the door open.

Paige turned to him, intending to thank him for driving her home and send him on his way, but she

hesitated. He stood with his hands in his pockets, his dark hair glistening with beads of rain.

"May I come in?" His voice was barely audible.

"Yes," she said, and stepped aside.

Paige toweled her hair as she walked around the front room checking the windows. Filled with sudden restless energy, she felt a need to keep moving.

Cody sat near the edge of a chair, leaning forward, his hands clasped before him.

She adjusted the venetian blinds and straightened the curtains, acutely aware that he was watching her, even more aware of his masculine presence in the room.

When she had done everything that she could to avoid looking at him, she simply stood gazing out at the rain.

"Do you want to talk about it?"

A minute went by before she answered. "Talk about what?"

"What you've been thinking about all the way from Leland."

Paige fingered the collar of her tunic. "I don't—"

"Why don't you admit it?"

The nearness of his voice startled her—she hadn't heard him cross the room—and she whirled to face him, saw the challenge in his eyes.

"What is it, Paige? What's bothering you?"

She shook her head stubbornly, and mentally sidestepped the questions that she'd been avoiding since . . .

"You can tell me." Cody held out his hand. "You've got to tell someone."

Paige closed her eyes, shutting him out. "No."

"I can help you."

"No one can . . ."

"But I know, Paige. I *know*."

She couldn't answer. Her throat ached and tears welled in her eyes.

"Let me."

He touched her bare arm and she shivered. She could feel the heat of him, the warmth of his breath on her skin. He was so near, so very near.

"Paige." It was a whisper, a plea, a promise.

Without conscious thought, she stepped into the circle of his arms, felt them close around her. Pressing her face against the damp fabric of his shirt, she clung to him as if her life depended on it.

A dream, she thought.

She stretched, arching her back, and felt the sensuous caress of air on her naked body. She reached for the sheet, but it was not at hand, and she opened her eyes.

The covers had been pushed off the end of the bed.

Cody Austin stood in the doorway, dressed only in khaki pants.

"Oh!" She sat up and pulled a pillow in front of her.

His smile was slow and lazy. "How do you feel?" He sat on the side of the bed.

Paige ran her hand through her hair, pushing it back from her face. "Fine," she said. She tucked her

legs beneath her and sat Indian-style so that the pillow would cover more of her.

Cody retrieved the bedcovers, offering them to her.
"You slept for a little while."

And before that?

A flash of memory, of the searing heat of his hands
on her body, the taste of his skin as she kissed the
hollow of his throat . . .

Paige blinked. It had not been a dream, then.

When she'd dressed, she went downstairs and
found him in the kitchen making coffee.

"The rain's stopped," he said.

She looked past him. Outside, the clouds were
beginning to part, and the sunlight spun a rainbow
from the mist.

A rainbow.

How long had it been since she'd seen a rainbow?

Unaccountably, tears blurred her vision and she
swallowed hard to keep back a cry of anguish and of
loss. Had she even looked at the sky since she was a
child? Really looked?

"Paige?" Cody's hand cradled her elbow, and he
led her to the table, made her sit down.

"What is wrong with me?" She wiped at her eyes
and attempted a smile. "I can't seem to stop."

Cody sat on his heels in front of her. "Don't even
try."

She shook her head. "I don't like myself like this."

"Because you're not in control?"

Her laughter surprised her. "Now you sound
like—"

307

"Like who?"

Alex, she thought, and felt a surge of guilt. "A friend of mine."

"I'm your friend, too." His hand was warm on her knee.

"Thank you," she said, "for being here."

"I meant it when I said I want to help you."

She put her hand over his. "I'm not sure you can. I'm not sure anyone can." She looked away, frowned. So much had happened. So much had changed. "I thought I could help myself, but . . . no one will tell me the truth."

"I will," he said.

Sixty-three

Noah straightened the collar of his dress uniform and studied his reflection in the mirror. Police work had changed him. There was little left of the idealistic young officer who'd promised to uphold the law, to protect, and to serve.

Idealism was hard to maintain when so many fellow policemen had fallen in pursuit of duty.

He put a strip of black tape across his badge, and wondered, as he always did, if someday he would be the one to make what the newspapers liked to call "the ultimate sacrifice."

"Don't think," the instructor at the academy had told them, "that because so much of the work is routine that that's the way it'll always be. Because you're cheating death, every day. *Every day.* You put on the uniform and you're a target."

He'd been shot at a couple of times, back in the city, although not with the regularity that was implied in cop movies. Just often enough to develop the borderline paranoia which was what kept most cops alive.

Ramos hadn't had time to learn the lesson.

But Noah wondered, if he had been the one on that dark road, whether the outcome would've been any different. Having seen the way the boy had lived, and knowing some of what the kid had been through, Noah thought he might have made a rookie's mistake.

Cheating death.

The cemetery was in sight of the church, and the mourners followed slowly behind the pallbearers. At the front of the procession, Rosalind, dressed in flowing black, walked stiffly, as if it hurt her to move.

A flute began to play, the notes almost crystalline in their purity, and a moment later a woman began to sing.

"Amazing grace, how sweet the sound . . ."

Noah looked up at the parting clouds and deep, vivid blue of the sky which showed through. The rain had cleaned the air, and he took a deep breath, felt a sweet relief at being alive.

A blackbird perched on a marble monument fluttered his wings as they passed by, but did not take flight.

"I once was lost, but now I'm found . . ."

Noah slowed his pace, looked at the bird and restrained an impulse to shoo it away.

"Was blind, but now I see."

When they reached the grave site, Rosalind was guided to a row of folding chairs to be seated.

She sat very still, her hands folded primly in her lap, her expression hidden by the black veil. Grim-

faced family members clustered around her protectively, the women with tearstained faces, the men with anger in their eyes.

"... *abiding faith in thee.*"

The young widow began to twist her wedding band around her finger.

Noah shifted his feet. The ground was spongy, still holding water, but they'd pumped out the grave, and the casket rested above the open hole.

The minister took his place at the graveside. A sudden gust of wind swirled around him, tugging at his vestments and carrying his words aloft, heavenward.

"Joseph ... husband to Rosalind, son of Estaban and Luisa, brother to Michael ..."

Rosalind moaned suddenly and bent forward from the waist, looking for a moment as if she would topple off the chair. "Joey," she cried. "Please, Joey."

Instantly those around her moved in, encompassing her in the fold, whispering reassurances. The minister hurried to her, taking her hands in his.

"No!" Her voice sounded raw, the death of her husband a still-bleeding wound. "It isn't fair ..." She pulled back, trying to free her hands, struggling to stand, when all at once the fight went out of her, and she sank bonelessly into the chair.

Noah looked away, his eyes coming to rest on the flag-draped coffin.

She's right, he thought; it isn't fair.

The flag had been folded and presented to

Rosalind, who now held it against her breast. Her head was bowed, but beneath the veil, Noah could see tears glistening on her face.

Noah forced his attention back to the service.

". . . a good man's grave is his Sabbath. Joseph Ramos is at rest."

The minister closed the Bible, bent down to gather a small handful of dirt which he then cast into the grave.

"Dust thou art, and unto dust shalt thou return."

It was over.

He stood apart from the others, watching as Rosalind was ushered into the black limousine. Talk was that she would not even go back to the house she'd shared with Joe, that by nightfall she would be in San Francisco.

A new life ahead of her.

Noah frowned.

The most anyone could do now for Joe Ramos was to find his killer.

It was time to go back to work.

Sixty-four

"I'll tell you . . ."

Paige was silent, waiting for him to continue, but her pulse had begun to race and her mouth had gone dry. In that moment she realized that she was afraid, that some part of her *didn't want to know*.

Lowering his voice, he said, "I believe I know who killed them."

"How can you? The police never—"

"The sheriff was part of it."

"No . . ." She couldn't make herself ask the only question that mattered, saying instead, "I don't believe it."

"Listen to me. Franklin Sinclair was bought off."

"What?"

"In 1960, he was in a financial bind. He owed a lot of money, and had gotten behind on his bills. I've been in his house. I've seen his records. He was near to being bankrupt."

Paige shook her head. "That doesn't prove anything."

"Not on its own. But a year later, he's miraculously out of debt. He suddenly has enough money to quit

313

his job and go to law school."

"It still isn't—"

"Proof? No, but it's part of the pattern."

"I don't understand."

Cody turned abruptly, walked to the other side of the kitchen, then faced her again at a distance. "There were a lot of people in this town who benefited from your parents' deaths. Your aunt . . . and Martin Wyatt."

Icy fingers clutched her heart and squeezed. "What do you mean?" she asked when she could trust herself to speak.

"I mean . . . your mother was a wealthy woman."

For a moment she could only stare at him, and then she didn't see him at all. Her thoughts turned inward, and she was bombarded by flashes of memory. . . .

Hiding in the parlor and hearing her grand-mother's voice—being surprised by the coolness of her tone—as she talked to the family attorney.

"Paige will be my only heir, and if I die before she reaches majority, she *must not*, under any circum-tances, go to live with her father's family."

"Certainly, Mrs. Chandler."

"You must see to it that they never get another dime of the Chandler money."

"Indeed."

"Oh, if only I'd known what Leigh had done . . . leaving her money to him. What could she have been thinking?"

The lawyer cleared his throat noisily. "There

might still be a way to fight it in court. It is a rather substantial inheritance."

"How? By implying that my daughter was not in her right mind? No . . . no. I'd rather let them have the damned money . . ."

At a gathering on her thirteenth birthday, she'd received a gift of pearl and diamond earrings from her aunt and uncle, who had been unable to attend. After excusing herself from their company, she had run to find a mirror to see how she looked.

"How kind of them," her grandmother's voice floated after her, "to buy her a gift with her own money."

The guests had laughed, but Paige, standing in the hallway, had not understood.

And much later, "You were robbed . . . they took everything . . . they took it all . . ."

Paige put her hand to her eyes, closing out the light.

". . . told everyone he'd inherited it, but it's more than a coincidence that he got his money at the same time your parents' estate was settled."

She forced herself to listen to what he was saying.

"Then, a few years later, he paid off the others . . ."

"Wait . . . what others?"

"Horace Goldstein and Bucky Hightower."

"Hightower? The man who—"

He nodded. "The one who was killed the other night."

Paige remembered what Martin had said about the killing, the callous, rather offhand manner in which he'd detailed the man's brutal murder, which brought her back to the focus of it all.

"Are you saying . . . are you saying that my uncle was paying these men to keep quiet about the murder of my parents?"

"I am. Every six months, like clockwork, he would make a withdrawal from his own account, and then, within a couple of days, Hightower and Goldstein would make deposits in their accounts. The amounts always match perfectly. I have copies of their bank records."

Stunned, she could only look at him blankly.

"And more than that . . ."

"More?" The pain in her voice was mirrored by the ache in her heart. She pressed her hands against her abdomen, as if by doing so, she could stop the wrenching pull of anguish that twisted her stomach.

Cody spoke quietly. "Martin may have been the one who killed your parents. Why else would he pay the townspeople to keep quiet?"

Sixty-five

Noah had only just walked into his office when the intercom buzzed. Loosening his tie, he crossed the room to the desk.

"Yeah?"

"Call on line three."

He grabbed the phone and punched the third button with a little more force than necessary.

"Clayton," he said.

"Sheriff," a female voice said, "you're a hard man to get ahold of."

He recognized the attempt at coyness but had no time to play games. "What can I do for you, Naomi?"

Her laughter was throaty, but there was a tremor of uncertainty behind it. "Many things, I'm sure. But that isn't why I called."

Noah sat on a corner of the desk and rifled through a small stack of messages, several of which were from Naomi. She was obviously anxious about something. "Why did you call?"

"I saw in the paper this morning that Martin Wyatt got . . . got shot."

He was surprised that the San Jose paper would

print a story from a small town like Tranquility; it seemed to him that they had enough of their own bad news. "That's right," he said.

"How is he, do you know?"

There was, Noah thought, genuine concern in her voice. "From what I hear, he's got an even chance of making it."

"Thank God. I called the hospital, but they wouldn't tell me anything, since I'm not family." She paused. "You are telling me the truth, aren't you?"

"Why wouldn't I?"

"I don't know . . . maybe she told you to lie to me."

Noah frowned. "She who?"

"Well, his wife—"

"Hold on. Why would Ellen Wyatt—"

Naomi spoke in a rush, "Maybe she found out about the money he gave me, and thought the wrong thing. There was nothing between us, I swear it, but women, *wives*, always jump to conclusions, and—"

"Naomi, hold on. What are you telling me?"

There was a long silence. In the background he could hear the hum of an air conditioner, and he pictured her, chain-smoking and drinking a morning beer, as she sat among the clutter in her front room.

"Naomi?"

"Shit. Me and my big mouth."

"You might as well tell me. You know I'll find out, one way or the other."

"Damn it!" she swore, but there was no heat to it, and he sensed that she was relieved at not having to keep it to herself. "All right. You know when I left

318

town? Martin gave me the money to go."

Noah recalled Wyatt telling him that he'd seen Naomi Hightower only once, on the day Bucky had beaten her and broken her nose. "You were friends?"

"We were friendly. I had been to him a couple of times after"—her voice hardened—"Bucky had proven himself a man by knocking me on my ass."

"And when you left, Wyatt gave you the money to go."

"Damn it, I know what you're thinking, but it wasn't like that at all!"

"I wasn't—"

"Martin Wyatt saved my life."

"Calm down," Noah said. "I'm not suggesting otherwise. I'm just trying to get the story straight."

"Well, the *story* is that he was decent to me, and he helped me when I had no one else to turn to."

He tried again. "Naomi, I'm not on a witch hunt. You called me, remember?"

She made a sound, a half-sob, and then sniffed. "I know, it's just . . . all my life people have thought the worst of me. And then I usually do exactly what they think I'll do . . . and hate myself for it."

At a loss, Noah said nothing.

"But this time, I was—what is it they say?—above reproach."

"I believe you."

"And I would hate for people to think bad of Martin, just because he helped me. He took a big risk, helping me out."

"What do you mean, risk?"

"If Bucky had found out, he would've been furious." Again, that hard edge entered her voice.

"Bucky wanted me to come crawling and begging back to him . . ."

"Still, wasn't it unlikely that Bucky would find out? I mean, I can't imagine them crossing paths very often, even in a small town like this."

"Oh, but they had some kind of business together."

"What?" Noah rubbed his forehead, trying to recall what Wyatt had said about knowing Bucky, that night he'd come by the office.

"Well, I don't know the details. . . . Bucky liked his secrets, as I told you. But . . ."

"Go on," he prompted.

"I was at Martin's office one time when Bucky came by. I thought he was looking for me, and I was ready to run, let me tell you. But it was money he was after. I heard him. . . . He must've been drunk, his voice was so loud."

Noah picked up a pencil and drew a dollar sign on one of Naomi's messages. "What did he say?"

"Something about getting an advance on his money. He was belligerent as hell, disrupted the whole office."

"Did you ask Dr. Wyatt about it?"

"No, I . . . I never did. Listen, I didn't want to get into all of this. It doesn't matter anyway, does it? Bucky's dead and, and . . ."

And, Noah thought, a deputy was killed and Wyatt—who'd told him that he knew Hightower only to say hello to—had gotten himself shot.

What the hell, he wondered crossly, is going on?

Sixty-six

They did not see her, did not even glance in her direction.

Felicity stood in plain view perhaps thirty feet from where they looked into each other's eyes.

She'd watched them drive up, watched as Cody—his shirt unbuttoned, as if he'd just gotten out of bed—got out of the low-slung car and ran around to the driver's side to open the door for her.

Now they faced each other, apparently oblivious to anyone else. Even from a distance, Felicity could tell that the lady doctor had been crying. Tears or not, she was undeniably beautiful.

"Let me come with you," Cody said.

She shook her head. "No. I need to . . . have to . . . do this on my own."

"What are you going to do?"

"I don't know."

He put his hands on her shoulders and pulled her toward him, enfolding her in his arms. They fit together like the last two pieces of a puzzle—inevitably.

Felicity felt her face burning and she turned,

wanting to run, although she knew she would not. Not yet.

She had to know, and she made herself look at them as she stepped backward, moving toward the trees along the side of the road.

Cody brushed her dark hair away from her face. "You'll come back?"

The tenderness in his voice made her ache with longing, and for a heartbeat, Felicity pretended that it was she he was talking to.

"Where else would I go?"

"I wish things were—"

She cut him off. "Wishing never changed anything." There was a haunted quality to her words, as if she had wanted to believe otherwise, but had been forced to accept a painful reality. It was a reality that Felicity knew well but she was surprised that someone so achingly beautiful had ever had a wish unanswered.

"Paige . . . it'll be all right."

There was no answer.

"Paige?"

"I don't know," she said haltingly, "what I'll do if . . . if it's true."

"Don't worry about a thing; I'll take care of whatever needs to be done."

"That's just it." Her voice was low and Felicity had to strain to hear. "I don't know what to do. Or what good it would do to do anything, after all this time. I can't seem to think straight."

"You'll know . . ."

He kissed her, cupping her face in his hands. Felicity looked down. She had worn her best dress,

322

a mint green silk with a white lace collar, but she felt ugly and graceless. Raising her hand, she smoothed the lace, her fingers tracing its delicate pattern.

What had she been thinking, coming here this way?

Had she truly imagined that, if she told him she was the one who'd left the journals at his door, he would do more than say thank you?

Had she really believed that, because she had given him her mother's journals, he would be so grateful to her that he wouldn't care if she was less than beautiful?

Had she actually danced in front of her mirror, admiring the way the skirt spun as she twirled, and pretending that he would think she *was* beautiful?

What foolish daydreams . . .

She ripped at the lace, which tore easily away from the silk bodice.

Felicity hurried off, walking at first and then, no longer caring if anyone saw her, she broke into a run.

Sixty-seven

Cody watched the Jaguar as it pulled away. If she looked back at him in the rearview mirror, she gave no sign. The car accelerated around a bend in the road and was gone.

"Damn!"

He pivoted and stalked toward the cottage. At the door he stopped, slammed his hand against the door frame, and then turned to look again down the road.

He should've gone with her.

There was no way of knowing what she would do on her own, or how she would react when she saw him. . . .

A headache had been building behind his eyes all morning, and now, fueled by his anger, it threatened to incapacitate him.

Inside, the stale air was almost palpable, a thick substance which was hard to breathe.

He left the door standing open and unlatched the windows, but it was several minutes before he detected any improvement in the air. By then his head felt as if it were splitting.

It was hard to think.

He couldn't afford to be ill right now; too much was at stake. He had to be in control. Had to.

In the bathroom he found the small vial of pills which he'd hidden inside a much larger bottle of aspirin. The cap fit tightly and he had to work at getting it open, but when he spilled the contents into the palm of his hand and he looked at the multicolored capsules and tablets, knowing what wonders they could perform, he felt a little better.

He picked out the small triangular tablets and popped them into his mouth, swallowing dry.

It was not long before they took effect.

Sitting at the kitchen table, he began to read through the journals after first putting them into chronological order.

There was no name on the books to identify the writer, but it quickly became clear that it was a woman.

October 2nd, 1960: Saw him today downtown. We could only nod "hello," but it was enough. I know he loves me. I haven't told him yet. Soon.

Cody skimmed through the pages, but the "him" wasn't identified. Others were, though, and he read with interest how Martin Wyatt had stirred things up by announcing that he would not take over Dr. Hutchinson's practice, but would instead move to the East Coast, where the "important" medical centers were located.

October 28th, 1960: Hotshot Wyatt, I guess he expects us to beg him to stay. But I wouldn't want him delivering MY baby. Our baby, I should say. I'll have to tell him soon, I know, but I'm afraid.

Small-town doings, he thought.

November 6th, 1960: I didn't have to tell him after all! He guessed! I forgot, he's been through this before. He bought me a red dress and shoes, for "after." It's more than I ever hoped for! He wants to marry me!!!

Suddenly impatient, he began flipping through the pages, seeing only fragments of phrases:

. . . has to be a boy . . .
. . . money won't buy . . .
. . . time to talk to her about a divorce . . .

Cody frowned, thumbed back through the pages, his eyes scanning for the name he'd half seen.
His frown deepened as he read.

Standing on the porch, he could hear the doorbell ringing inside the big house. He adjusted the straps of his backpack, which, under the combined weight of the journals, were digging into his shoulders.
Almost certain that Charlotte Sinclair wasn't home, he nonetheless waited, pushing the bell at minute intervals and wondering what he would say if

she did answer the door. He could ask her to use the phone, he supposed, or borrow a wrench, or remind her of her promise to show him the slides from her last cruise. . . .

But there was no response from within the house, and after a careful glance at the surrounding area, he used the key she had given him to get in.

The quiet was absolute; he couldn't detect even the usual sounds a house makes as it settles, the creaks and groans used by filmmakers to set the mood for their high-tech horrors. Silence, he thought, was spooky, even in the middle of the day.

He closed the door behind him.

The entrance to the basement stairway was secreted behind the floor-to-ceiling shelf in the kitchen pantry. He'd never have found it if he hadn't, weeks ago, come upon the blueprints in Franklin Sinclair's files while looking for documents from the Brown case.

The stairway itself was steep, the steps narrow, and he had to hold on to a railing as he made his way down. In the dim light provided by the overhead fixture, he could see crates and boxes lined neatly along the far wall.

To the right, an old-fashioned steamer trunk sat open, its contents—mostly old clothes by the look of it—spilling out and onto the floor.

But what he was interested in was the kiln.

The widow Sinclair had a habit of self-indulgence, and during one numbing monologue she'd told him about taking up the "throwing" of pottery. She admitted readily that her enthusiasm had waned when she found that making even the simplest bowls

took considerable work.

A blob of red clay, hardened now, sat in the middle of a turntable.

Cody moved past the small work area and crossed to the kiln itself, shrugging off the backpack as he went.

A single glance confirmed its suitability: it would do nicely.

He worked the fire until it was white hot, and when he tossed the first of the books in, it smoldered for only a moment before bursting into flames.

One by one, he burned the journals.

In his mind, he could still see the words written in that precise hand:

> *If only he could make her realize that it would be better for everyone—her precious Paige included—if she agreed to the divorce.*

A pinprick of pain stabbed at his eyes and he closed them, bracing himself against it, but the expected relapse did not occur.

He was in control.

He would not allow anyone to change that.

Sixty-eight

From the cover of the trees, Stephen could see the front of the house.

Although he stood very still, he felt as though, beneath his skin, his muscles were contracting and flexing, readying themselves for what was to come.

Feeling a ripple of movement across his forearm, Stephen kept his eyes determinedly on the house, not wishing to see the gleaming wetness of exposed muscle and tendon. . . .

Muscle and tendon that would dry in a hundred days or a hundred years, making him into a leather man . . .

Leather man.

His throat constricted and he made a sound, a high-pitched wail like that of an injured animal. He bit his tongue as hard as he could stand, stopping only when he tasted blood.

It was a trick he had learned at that place, to keep himself from crying. To keep *them* from sticking needles into him.

Stephen sucked at his tongue. The blood always

made his mouth fill with saliva, and he had to swallow repeatedly, gagging once or twice.

His eyes had begun to water and he blinked to bring the world back in focus.

All at once, he couldn't recall why he had come here, and he looked around in confusion, then began backing away from the trees. Sunlight filtered through the branches and onto his face. Light, shadow, light, shadow.

He dropped to the ground, breathing rapidly.

Voices.

Covering his head with both hands, he pressed his face against the leaves and dirt, and waited for them to start grabbing and clutching at him.

Voices.

"If you don't tell me, I can't help you."

"I want to help you . . ."

"We can help . . ."

". . . help you . . . help you . . ."

Stephen moved his hands to his ears and rolled over on his back, his mouth open but soundless while his cries echoed in his head.

He welcomed the darkness when it overcame him.

Something touched his face and Stephen sat upright, brushing at his eyes and mouth. When he brought his hand away from his mouth, he saw dark specks of dried blood, but he was not frightened.

He remembered.

Remembered why he had come and what he had

to do.

Crawling on his hands and knees, he made his way back to where he had dropped the paper bag. After reassuring himself that the matches were still inside, he began to pull handfuls of dry grass from the ground, making a neat pile.

Sixty-nine

At midday, the hospital hummed with activity. In contrast to the night before, the hallways were brightly lit and filled with people. Over the intercom, the operator's disinterested voice issued a continual litany of names and numbers.

For the first time in her life, Paige felt as if the hospital was an alien environment. All that had been familiar to her, she now perceived as foreign, somehow unreal, an illusion with no substance.

An illusion, because despite all the purpose and dedication and noble motives, there were no true miracles being performed.

It was hopeless, she thought, to fight death; death would always win. What they—and before now she—thought of as victories were in truth only postponements. . . .

How had she fooled herself for so long?

Walking toward the elevator, she looked downward, not wanting to meet anyone's eyes.

* * *

She went first to Coronary Care.

During the day, admittance to the unit was restricted, requiring that she check in at the reception desk in the waiting room. The sliding glass window was open and rock music drifted out.

The secretary was biting into a powdered donut when Paige came up to the desk, and she smiled whitely before wiping her mouth on a napkin.

"Sorry . . ." She chewed and swallowed. "I didn't have breakfast. Can I help you?"

"I'm Dr. Brown, Ellen Wyatt's niece. She was admitted last night. I'd like to see her."

"Umm, right." At the 'doctor,' the woman's attitude had changed subtly, taking on an air of deference. "Let me check for you." As she got to her feet, she popped the remainder of the donut into her mouth and then turned away.

Paige waited.

A moment later, the secretary returned, her expression unreadable. "I'm sorry, Dr. Brown," she said, "but the doctor is with Mrs. Wyatt and he asked if you would mind waiting?"

Paige looked past the secretary. Frosted glass double-doors separated the waiting room from the patient area, but behind them she could see shapes moving about. There was no urgency in their movements, nothing that would indicate a crisis underway.

"I'll wait," she said.

Twenty minutes later the secretary informed her that it would probably be another half hour before she would be allowed in to see Ellen.

"They're taking x-rays and doing an EKG. If you want to go to the cafeteria for coffee, I can have you paged."

"That won't be necessary," she said softly, "I have something else to do."

"Dr. Wyatt's been moved into isolation," the ICU charge nurse said, glancing up from a precariously balanced stack of charts.

Paige frowned. "Is he all right?"

The nurse inclined her head. "I believe he's stable, but Dr. Park is quite concerned about the possibility of infection, and he doesn't want to take any chances."

"I see."

"Did you want to talk to Dr. Park? I'm sure he's still in the hospital. I can try and find him for you."

"Don't bother; I imagine I'll see him before I leave."

The nurse started to speak but was interrupted by a ringing phone. Paige turned from the desk and walked toward the isolation room.

After dressing in a sterile gown, mask, and gloves, she went inside.

The room was air-conditioned, but Paige felt sweat trickle down her back as she went to stand at Martin's bedside.

His eyes were closed and he did not stir as she came

near. They had taken him off the respirator, and he was breathing on his own. The cardiac monitor showed a normal sinus rhythm, and a digital display showed pulse and blood pressure rates that were only slightly elevated.

He was doing well.

Paige made herself look at his face.

She held on to the bed railing, her fingers tightening around the cool metal.

Lines etched the skin around his mouth, and his thin lips turned down at the corners. Staring at him, she found herself remembering his bitter smile as he told her of Ellen's desire to have a child. It had disturbed her then, but now, looking back, she wondered at the icy interior of a man who could be so unfeeling to the woman he professed to love. What kind of a man was he?

Had he only stayed with Ellen because of the money she'd inherited from her brother?

Was Cody right? *"He may have been the one who killed your parents."*

Had Martin Wyatt murdered her parents? Had Martin Wyatt stabbed her father? Had he plunged the knife, still wet with her father's blood, into her mother's chest?

A sick feeling of rage threatened to overwhelm her. So many times, over the years, she had treated stabbing victims, and always, through force of will, she had managed to keep from making the mental connection between their wounds and those of her parents.

But no more. With sudden clarity, she visualized

338

them, lying on the kitchen floor, savagely wounded, blood pooled around them.

Paige took a step backward, still holding on to the railing, and closed her eyes.

It would be so easy to kill him now.

So very easy.

Seventy

Noah steered into the curve, accelerated, and felt the tires spinning as they slid through the loose dirt and gravel before finally taking hold. Fifty yards ahead of him, the fire department's tanker truck lumbered along, its siren screaming, drowning out his own.

Smoke billowed into the air, where it hovered like a storm cloud, a miniature, deadly version of those in the sky.

"Come on," he said.

The tanker swerved, went off the road, cutting a corner to the Goldstein driveway. With it out of his way, he could see that the house was fully engulfed in flames.

On the lawn, several of the firemen struggled to restrain a flailing victim . . . Stephen.

Noah pulled up, slammed the gear shift into park, and jumped out of the car before it had fully stopped. He started to unsnap his holster, but coming closer, he saw that there was no need.

The boy was being held to the ground as one of the firemen cut through his clothes. He had been burned,

341

and on his arms and face the skin hung loose, sloughing off. While Noah watched, they stripped him bare and then wrapped him in a cotton sheet. Using the sheet to lift him, they loaded him onto a stretcher.

A second later, kneeling at the boy's side, a medic deftly inserted an IV needle into a badly blistered arm.

They didn't wait for an ambulance, but loaded him into the medic's van.

Throughout all of it, the boy never made a sound.

Noah felt the heat of the fire on his back as he watched them drive away, and shivered as he imagined what it must have felt like, being burned that way.

Horace Goldstein showed up about ten minutes later, still wearing his grocer's apron.

The fire captain got to him first, and as Noah crossed the yard, he noted the expression on the old man's face stayed the same.

Goldstein was angry.

Just that, anger. The man showed no shock and no concern for his son.

". . . did it on purpose," Goldstein was saying as Noah came up to them.

"Now, we don't know that for a fact, Horace, and we won't know for a while yet."

"I damned well *do* know it." Goldstein's eyes flicked to Noah and then widened in alarm.

Noah reached and grabbed him by the collar, shaking him as he pushed the man backward.

"Hey!" the fire captain said.

"This is police business." He tightened his hold on Goldstein and then abruptly pushed him away. Goldstein stumbled but didn't fall.

"What the—"

Noah kept his voice low. "You bastard. I've about had all I'm gonna take of you."

"What did I do?" Goldstein's eyes were wide with fear. "I swear, I didn't—"

"Shut up! I'll tell you when you can talk, and when I do, you'd better tell the truth, because I'm getting sick and tired of being lied to."

Goldstein opened his mouth as if to protest and then thought better of it. Keeping his eyes fixed on Noah, he tried to straighten his collar.

"I want to know what's going on."

"Wha—what's going on?" Goldstein gestured wildly. "My house is burning down!"

Noah shook his head. "That isn't what I want to hear." He took a step closer to Goldstein; he could smell the man's sweat even over the strong acrid odor of smoke.

Goldstein staggered backward, but he was up against the side of the patrol car. He gripped the side mirror and braced his heels in the dirt. "I don't know what you want to hear . . . I don't know . . . Jesus, Sheriff . . . I . . . " His mouth flapped open but nothing else came out.

"The truth." Noah narrowed his eyes. "Remember that? Or has it been so long since you've told the truth that you don't know what it is?"

"Whatever you want . . ."

"Tell me about Stephen."

343

Goldstein blanched. "What about him?"

"You think he set this fire . . . I think he shot a cop. I think he may have done a lot of things. And I want you to tell me what the hell's wrong with him."

"The doctors—"

"I don't want to hear what the doctors say. . . . They've lost their credibility, as far as I'm concerned. I can go to court if I want his medical records, but I have a feeling that whatever I found there, wouldn't be the truth. They only know what you told them . . . and you've been lying right along."

Goldstein wiped the back of his hand across his mouth and then tried to nod, a spastic movement that made him look as though his neck was broken.

"The truth," Noah warned.

Panic showed in Goldstein's eyes. "The truth."

At first Goldstein's voice was so quiet that Noah could barely hear him.

"My wife, you know, Susanna, she died of it. It was a long time ago. Oh, she was beautiful. A woman that beautiful, you can't believe that anything is wrong with her. But she was like him." He nodded to himself. "It broke my heart to see what she turned into. A crazy woman."

Noah didn't speak, but watched the old man closely.

If Goldstein was aware of Noah's presence, he gave no sign. His eyes were blank, unfocused.

"Schizophrenia, they call it. They told me that Stephen might not get it; back then they weren't sure if it was hereditary or not. Now they think it is." His

mouth twitched and he bared his teeth in a rictal smile that was horrible to look at. "Oh, they've learned so much, those doctors!"

"How did she die?"

The smile faded. "She had a reaction to the medication they gave her. She died on the floor, foaming at the mouth like an animal. And you know what they did, to try and save her? They shot her full of more drugs." Hatred shone in his eyes. "You should've seen what they did to her there. When I saw her body . . ."

Noah waited a moment before asking, "And Stephen?"

The emotion drained from Goldstein's face. "When he was ten. He was all right until he was ten."

"What happened then?"

Goldstein was shaking his head. "I told him, bury the body, but he was afraid to go back there, afraid that someone would see him . . . so we left it. He said nobody would ever find it, not in a hundred years."

"What body? Who was afraid?"

For the first time, Goldstein looked directly at Noah. "We killed a man, back in 1960. Killed him and left him in the woods to rot. Vigilantes, we were. The sheriff let him go and we found him and killed him."

"Wait a minute. Who—"

"Stephen loved to play in the woods. Spent all his time there. I should've known that sooner or later he'd wander up the hill . . ."

"He found the body?"

"Fell over it, running through the woods. The man had been dead twenty years. His skin was like

tanned leather, dried up. Didn't look human. When the boy fell on him, the body kind of came apart." Incredibly, Goldstein laughed. "The arms stayed put—he was nailed to the tree—but the rest just collapsed. The head dropped off into the boy's lap, and was grinning up at him. Scared the sanity right out of that boy."

Noah stared hard at Goldstein. "Nailed to the tree? The way Hightower was?"

"I suppose so," he said dreamily. "Kind of delayed justice, Bucky getting killed that way. It was his idea to do that."

Questions crowded Noah's mind as he tried to make sense of what Goldstein was telling him. "Who was this man?"

Goldstein shrugged. "Don't recall. Just someone who Roger Brown had hired to help him dig a new well. He was seen running from the Brown place the night they got killed. Frank hauled him in, but then let him go. Said he had no reason to hold him. No proof."

"So you and Hightower—"

"And a couple of others," he said hurriedly. "It wasn't just us. We had a notion that we had all the *proof* we needed. Hell, he was the only outsider in town. Who else could've done it?"

Noah wondered if Horace Goldstein hadn't lost his grip on sanity long before Susanna or Stephen had. "So . . . you killed a man."

"We did. But then . . ." his voice faltered.

"Go on."

"It turned out that he hadn't done it . . ."

"Wait! I thought those murders were never solved."

"Oh, they were solved, all right. But the sheriff and Martin Wyatt took it upon themselves to hush it all up. Keeping secrets. So Bucky and I, we decided we could keep a secret too. Then later, when we saw what Wyatt was doing for Frank, the money and all, we thought we'd get in on a good thing. It was only fair."

Noah wanted to knock the self-satisfied, self-righteous expression off Goldstein's face.

Instead he said, "There is no statute of limitations on murder. You have the right to remain silent . . ."

Seventy-one

Paige leaned against the back of the elevator. Her pulse was racing and she felt light-headed, as though she might faint.

A nurse touched her arm. "Are you okay?"

"Yes, I'm fine." She wanted to smile but she was afraid that it wouldn't hold, and she would wind up in tears. When the elevator doors opened, she got off as unobtrusively as she could.

It wasn't the right floor, but she realized that she needed a few minutes to get herself together before she went to see Ellen. Needing to be alone, she sought refuge in the stairway. Somewhere above her, she could hear footsteps, but they were not coming in her direction, and a moment later all was quiet.

She sat on the cold cement steps and tried to collect her thoughts.

Nothing in her life had prepared her for the intensity of emotion she'd felt as she looked upon the face of the man who might have killed her parents. For a very long time she had succeeded in insulating herself from strong feelings, but that insulation had been torn away, and she felt raw to the bone.

She wrapped her arms around her legs, hugging them to her, and closing her eyes, she rested her head on her knees.

"What now?" she asked herself. "What do I do now?"

Ellen looked markedly better. They'd taken her off the respirator, and her eyes fluttered open as Paige approached the bed.

She had seen this before in cardiac patients; a rapid, dramatic improvement, without apparent clinical cause. Yet she had also seen, almost as often, a patient rally briefly before slipping into death.

"How is he?" Her aunt's voice was raspy, an aftereffect of the endotrachial airway. "Have you seen him?"

Paige nodded. "I just came from there. He'll be all right. Try not to worry."

"Noah told me . . . you saved Martin's life."

"The surgeon . . ."

"If you hadn't been there . . . he wouldn't have made it to the hospital . . ."

"No one can know that for sure."

Ellen blinked, and tears pooled beneath her eyes. She spoke with an obvious effort. "You saved him, and bless you for that."

Paige looked away, unable to answer. How could she answer when half an hour ago she'd come close to killing the man whose life she'd saved? She still wasn't sure why she had walked out of his room. . . .

"What . . . is it, Paige?"

Her throat tightened and she took a deep breath.

"Paige?"

She met her aunt's eyes. "Aunt Ellen, I have to ask you something . . ."

"Yes, I know." Ellen's smile was infinitely sad. "There's so little time left. The doctors don't say, but I know." She raised one hand and waved it feebly. "But never mind. I must tell you. I must tell you before . . . it's too late. Because, you see, Martin did it for me."

Paige took a sharp breath.

Ellen closed her eyes tightly and then wiped at her face with shaking fingers. "He didn't want to . . . he's a principled man . . . but I . . . I talked him into it."

"What?" The word came out harsher than she'd intended, but she could no longer stand not knowing. "What did Martin do?"

"He . . . falsified . . . the death certificates."

Confused, Paige shook her head. "I don't understand."

The words were a whisper: "Your mother wasn't . . . murdered. She killed herself after . . . she stabbed your father."

Seventy-two

Paige stood at the doorway of her parents' room. It was nearing dusk, the shadows waiting in the corners for the night.

How long she had been standing there, she didn't know.

Somehow, she'd made her way out of the hospital and all the way home. It scared her a little that she could drive that distance without being aware of anything around her.

She rested her head against the door frame and allowed her eyes to close.

How could it be, she wondered, that she felt nothing?

Downstairs, a door closed and someone started up the steps.

"Paige?"

She recognized his voice, but did not turn.

"What's happened?"

Paige shook her head. "It doesn't matter. It's over. Nothing matters anymore."

Cody touched her face, wiping away tears she had unknowingly cried. "Tell me what happened."

She didn't want to talk about, didn't want to *think* about it. But she no longer had the strength to hold it in.

"Everything . . . it was a lie."

He frowned. "I don't—"

"The murders," she said bitterly, "the damned murders that haunted my dreams for *twenty-six years*. And somewhere in my mind, I blamed myself because I didn't see the man who ran away from the house. Because I didn't see the killer. I thought I had failed them, failed my parents . . ."

"No . . ." He reached and took her hands in his, pulling her forward so that they were standing only inches apart.

She searched his eyes, saw her own pain reflected there, and then let go. . . .

"My father was having an affair," she said. "They'd been fighting, arguing, for several days. That day, for some reason, it got out of hand. My mother," her voice dropped to a whisper, "killed my father, and then she killed herself."

"No," Cody said, a stricken look on his face, "no."

For a moment the hurt was so profound that she felt as though she couldn't breathe, and she pulled her hands from his. She hugged herself tightly and gasped at the crushing weight of the truth.

Paige sat on the side of the bed and accepted the glass that Cody held out to her.

Night had fallen and the room was veiled in darkness, the only light coming from the moon, which had risen full and yellow in the eastern sky.

354

She drank the water. Its coolness soothed her throat.

Cody paced the room, not looking at her.

Something had changed with the coming of the night. *He* had changed.

She watched him, vaguely disturbed. He moved like a cat. A big cat . . . trapped in a cage.

He no longer seemed to be aware of her, or aware of anything other than his own thoughts, but when she reached to put the glass down, he whirled to face her. His eyes locked onto hers and she saw that his pupils were constricted, almost pinpoint.

"We'll have to kill them," he said calmly.

Shock kept her silent.

"Have to." He nodded once and turned away. "It would've been better if they both had died, but they didn't and now we'll have to kill them."

Paige was afraid to look away from him. Keeping her voice neutral, she asked, "Why?"

At first she thought he hadn't heard her. He crossed the room, stopping in front of the window before facing her again.

"The story," he said simply. And then he smiled.

The moon was no longer framed in the window.

He had stopped pacing and now stood to the left of the window, looking out. Occasionally he nodded to himself, but he hadn't spoken in over an hour.

Paige watched him and wondered what he would do if she got up from the bed.

She wondered if she was fast enough to get out the

355

door, down the stairs and out of the house before he caught her. More than that, she wondered if getting out of the house would do any good. There were no close neighbors, and she would have to run a good distance to find help.

What would he do to her if he caught her?

He was, she thought, irrational. Judging from the look of his eyes, he was on something, probably amphetamines. That made him unpredictable, and possibly dangerous.

For a while he had rambled on about his "story," and it had become clear to her that for him, story was all. There was not even a hint of regret in his voice as he talked about killing Ellen and Martin. They were characters. Not real. Dispensable.

Paige understood then; to him, she was only one of the characters in his story.

"I've got the perfect ending," he'd said.

If she ran, and he caught her, would she die in the end?

At the window, he smiled, and then his lips moved rapidly, without sound. He held himself rigid, as if, in his drug-heightened state of awareness, he could feel the air pressing in on him.

From the corner of her eye she could see the door and the top of the stairway.

Unbidden, the image of her mother filled her mind.

Paige shivered, tried to suppress the vision of her parents struggling on the stairs, her mother raising the knife and bringing it down. . . .

She blocked it out, forced herself to concentrate on the distance between the bed and the door.

If she made it outside, she knew where she could hide. Under the cover of darkness, he would never find her.

She waited until she saw him close his eys.

For an instant she thought that her legs would refuse to move, but then she was running, her heart pounding as she raced through the door.

She took the stairs three at a time, trusting her instincts in the dark, and slipping only once, midway down, but saving herself from falling by grabbing onto the rail.

Her breathing was so loud that she couldn't tell where he was, and she sprinted to the door.

It was locked and she threw the dead bolt, expecting every second to feel his hands grabbing her from behind. Even so, she set the lock so that it would catch if she managed to shut it after her.

And then the door was open and she was out.

In two steps she was across the porch and she leaped off, hit the ground running. . . .

When she got to the acacia trees, she changed direction, running along the periphery of the grove rather than deeper into the woods. When she was a hundred yards to the left of where she'd entered, she stopped and pressed herself against a tree.

She had heard him come out of the door, the thud of his footsteps on the porch, but she hadn't dared to turn and see how far he was behind. Now she positioned herself so that she could view the yard.

He had apparently made it to the trees.

Although her lungs were straining, she took and

held a deep breath. Her pulse hammered in her ears, but over it she heard the crackle of twigs and undergrowth.

Away. He was going away.

Without hesitation, she found hand and footholds, and started to climb the tree. The bark dug into the palms of her hands and she scraped her face, but she fought her way up off the ground and into a sheltering vee.

She pressed her back against the sturdy limb, braced her feet, and reached up to hold on to a branch.

Shutting her eyes, she focused on slowing her breathing, afraid that if he realized she'd changed direction, he would stand still to listen for her movements, and would hear her labored breathing instead.

Gradually, she quieted.

Around her, the woods had grown silent.

Where is he, she wondered.

Her muscles ached both from running and from the forced stillness of her body.

To the east, the sky had begun to lighten.

She had not seen him come out of the woods.

He could be anywhere, she knew. He could be hidden behind a tree ten feet away, or all the way around on the other side of the property. He could've come out of the woods behind the cover of the house.

She looked toward the Jag parked in the drive.

The keys to it were in the house, but there was an extra set in a small metal case in the left rear fender

well. If she could get to the car, it would take only seconds to retrieve the keys and open the door.

But the way the car was parked meant that if he was still on this side of the yard, she would be in view while she searched for the key.

Paige frowned, looked back at the deep woods. He could be standing in that gloom, waiting for her to make a move. If so, he would see her the minute she jumped down from the tree. And it would be a race again, to see if he could reach her before she made it to the car.

Still, she didn't have much choice. When daylight came, he would be able to see her anyway. Her hiding place would be good only for another hour at best.

She was certain that he'd kill her if he had a chance.

The ground beneath the tree was fairly level, although overgrown with weeds. There was no exposed root, nothing to trip her up.

Paige rubbed her thighs, massaging the cramped muscles, and then slowly lowered her legs over the side of the limb. It looked to be about eight feet to the ground.

She jumped.

A sharp pain shot up her right heel and into the calf of her leg.

Ignoring it, she scrabbled forward, bent over until she cleared the remainder of the trees, and then straightened, knowing that she could run faster upright.

She heard nothing.

At the car she slid, felt the fabric rip over her knees, and then gravel dug into her flesh. She grabbed hold of the fender well and thrust her arm up beneath the

tire and the car body.

As her fingers closed around the magnetic case, she heard thrashing, the sound of brush being pushed aside.

But she had the case, had it open, and she knocked the keys out of the case, into her hand.

The key fit smoothly into the lock.

"Paige!" he yelled.

She didn't turn, but pulled the door open and flung herself inside. She yanked the door shut, locked it, and only then looked to see where he was.

He had stopped perhaps fifteen feet away.

Their eyes held.

Paige turned the key in the ignition, put the car in reverse, and backed up.

He stood there, looking after her as she drove off.

Epilogue

Noah walked along the corridor to the interrogation room where Paige Brown was waiting to give her statement. At the door he stopped, listening for a moment to her soft voice as she talked with the stenographer. He opened the door.

She glanced up at him. Her hair was disheveled and she had an abrasion under her right cheekbone, but it was her eyes that drew his attention.

He saw the pain, the haunted look of loss, but there was also a kind of relief in those gray eyes.

"How are you doing?" he asked, sitting at the table across from her.

"Better."

"We're looking for him, but you know there's not much we can do." He shook his head. "I can charge him with breaking and entering, but not much else. The threats he made won't count in a court of law."

"I know." She ran a hand through her hair. "I'm not even sure anymore whether he really intended to kill anyone. It all may have been . . . a bad dream."

Noah hesitated. "I'm sorry. For what you had to go through." He nodded to the stenographer. "We'd

better get on with this; you must be tired."

"I don't know where to start." There was a tremor in her voice, but she attempted a smile.

"Wherever you want."

There was a long silence.

Finally, she began to talk, speaking slowly but with control. "I don't know all of it . . . but the real beginning . . . was in the fall of 1960. I was eight. My father had an affair with a woman named Lenore O'Hara. I understand that she still lives here in town. She . . . became pregnant."

Paige held her hands out in front of her, palms up, and Noah saw the contusions, fought back an impulse to take her hands in his.

"Because of that, my father and . . . my mother . . . began to fight. I heard some of their arguments, although I didn't understand what they were fighting about."

Noah leaned forward, resting his arms on the table and steepling his hands.

"I've been told that my mother killed my father, and then killed herself." She looked at him, as though to gauge the effect of her words.

That agreed, essentially, with what Goldstein had told him, so he merely nodded. "Go on."

"I had seen a man, running from the house, but . . . he had nothing to do with the . . . their deaths. My aunt said that he was questioned and let go, supposedly because of lack of evidence, but really . . . what really happened was that they determined that my mother . . ." Her voice trailed off and she closed her eyes.

Noah saw no point in telling her that the man

she'd seen had himself been killed, and that that killing had spawned two others. She had enough to bear.

"So." When she looked at him again, her eyes were bright with unshed tears. "From what I was told, I gather that the decision was made to keep the truth a secret. Both to protect me . . . and to keep the courts from declaring my mother's will invalid."

He frowned. "I don't understand."

"My mother had left her money and property to my father. His will left everything to his sister. Ellen. She was . . . my aunt was also pregnant. She and Martin were deeply in debt from his years in medical school, and desperate for money. She knew that I was . . . well provided for . . . by my grandparents' wills . . . and trusts. She convinced Martin to falsify my mother's death certificate."

"So Ellen Wyatt was the beneficiary?"

"My father . . . died . . . first. But he had . . ." She paused and took a deep breath before continuing. "He had nothing of his own. So my mother . . . had to be the one . . . they needed her to be the one who died first."

"Determining time of death wasn't that exact back then. It's not that accurate now."

Her voice was a whisper. "Enough time went by, between when she . . ."

The stenographer had stopped writing, and there was no sound in the room.

". . . I guess it took her a while . . . to get up the nerve to . . . kill herself."

Noah touched her hand. Her fingers closed around his, but she did not look at him.

"They were also . . . worried . . . that, if the truth came out, the courts would question my mother's . . . mental state . . . and the trust would revert back to me. So they kept their secrets . . . for all those years."

He felt a dull anger in the pit of his stomach, but knew this was not the time to vent it.

"The sheriff was in on it. And I guess, a few others."

A small town, he thought. Small-town people taking care of their own.

"Anyway . . . it was a long time ago." Gently, she withdrew her hand from his and sat back in her chair. "It *is* over, now."

Noah heard the question beneath the words. There were a lot of people who'd sidestepped the law in hiding the truth, but all of them had paid a price for what they'd done. What would be gained by cutting open old wounds?

"It's over," he agreed. "Come on, I'll take you home."

MYSTERIES TO KEEP YOU GUESSING
by John Dickson Carr

CASTLE SKULL (1974, $3.50)
The hand may be quicker than the eye, but ghost stories didn't hoodwink Henri Bencolin. A very real murderer was afoot in Castle Skull—a murderer who must be found before he strikes again.

IT WALKS BY NIGHT (1931, $3.50)
The police burst in and found the Duc's severed head staring at them from the center of the room. Both the doors had been guarded, yet the murderer had gone in and out *without having been seen*!

THE EIGHT OF SWORDS (1881, $3.50)
The evidence showed that while waiting to kill Mr. Depping, the murderer had calmly eaten his victim's dinner. But before famed crime-solver Dr. Gideon Fell could serve up the killer to Scotland Yard, there would be another course of murder.

THE MAN WHO COULD NOT SHUDDER (1703, $3.50)
Three guests at Martin Clarke's weekend party swore they saw the pistol lifted from the wall, levelled, and shot. *Yet no hand held it*. It couldn't have happened—but there was a dead body on the floor to prove that it had.